SALVAGING THE ARCTIC WRECK

THE FORGOTTEN PLANET

BOOK 3

KATE MACLEOD

CHAPTER 1

Lafayette Eloi had spent the first eighteen years of her life in the same village. The cluster of a few dozen houses and public buildings had been her entire world. The extent of that world had been easily defined, all within the circle of the horizon where the flat plains of grassy fields surrounding her village met the blue of the sky above.

In that world, the tallest thing she had ever seen was the tree that stood at the heart of the village. When she was little, she used to lie down under its branches and look up at the glimpses of indigo sky beyond it and try to imagine anything more immense than its umbrella-like canopy. She had tried to imagine touching anything that felt older than its trunk, a trunk so thick three children pressed against it could just reach each other's hands.

Lafayette had tried so hard then, to imagine taller things or older things. Because she had known such things existed. She had read about them in her parents' books and journals. She had listened to both of them tell her stories of such things. But she had never quite succeeded in making her mind really picture what it would be like, to look up at something taller. To touch something older.

A lot of things had changed for Lafayette in the last few months.

She had walked a distance that she knew from maps represented a good fourth of the way across the known world. She had watched one kind of grass grow sparser and other, newer grasses grow more dominant as she walked from region to region. She had seen the snow-capped peaks of mountains, little more than a smudge off to the west, for days and days as she traveled north. Her path never brought her any closer to them, not before the grasses around her grew so tall they and the horizon they dominated were lost to view.

Then she had turned east, heading to the very center of all the maps. Heading to the capital city where her parents had met as students. She had heard all their stories. She had seen all the pictures in history books of what it had once looked like. She had seen drawings of the fields and grassy hills that had once stretched for kilometers between the last of the buildings and the domineering height of those walls that ringed the city from the highest elevation.

The stone walls that had once contained everyone who lived within the capital with space to spare were overrun with people and their structures now. More than that, the city she had seen with her own eyes had started long before she had even reached those walls. Village after village had dotted the landscape all around those walls, as humanity burst the containment of that ring of stone and sprawled into the grasslands all around.

She had learned to speak dialects she had only heard of before. She had tasted food so exotic she had never even read descriptions of it before.

She had seen the remains of two of the spaceships that had brought her ancestors to this world centuries before. She had touched their metal hulls and felt the indescribable age of them, feeling almost like they were sleeping, waiting to be found again.

Her father had made it his life's work to find them. And he had brought Lafayette along when he had finally, at long last, succeeded.

She still thought of her younger self, lying under the village tree and looking past its boughs into the sky beyond. But her feelings about that tree had changed so much.

After seeing that first spaceship, half-buried in its own crash crater and covered with dense tangles of jungle, Lafayette had a hard time remembering when that village tree had felt so tall. Even the trees in that jungle that had grown around the crashed ship had dwarfed her old, familiar tree.

She had thought on that horrid day when she and her half-robot dog Kora had been forced to leave that crater behind—the day that derelict of a ship had launched itself back up into space with her father still trapped on board—that she was numb now to any sense of wonder. All the amazing things she had seen on that ship, it had all been a part of the same thing that had taken her father from her. And so soon after her mother had died, to lose her father too had been so much to bear.

That numbness had taken the edge off her grief and despair, which had been necessary. She had needed to not be feeling those things while she and Kora had trekked across kilometer after kilometer of hot grasslands, hiding from strangers who might be bandits and trading everything her father had left behind with her for just a bit more food, so she could continue walking to the capital. But there had always been a tiny voice in the back of her mind that worried about that numbness.

Not that she wanted to feel that grief and despair again. She still wasn't ready. And, in the last day, she had added another loss to her personal toll. Her father's mentor, Uche Okafo, had taken her in and promised to help her, only to be arrested by Central Planning and disappeared into one of their many secret prisons. She didn't know if she'd ever see him again, let alone her father trapped up in space, on a ship locked in orbit, a ship he couldn't control.

No, it was too soon to not feel numb yet. And until she had no choice but to give her father up as lost to her, it would remain too soon to feel all those things.

But she did worry that the numbness might be blocking her from feeling wonder like she should.

Certainly, she had marveled at the city, even as its sheer size overwhelmed her, and its throngs of humanity almost frightened her at times. The strange but amazing food she had tasted in the last few days had made an impression on her as well.

And that sense of marvel had only grown when she had realized that what had appeared to be a tall metal pillar in the center of the city, one with the government buildings perched atop of it, was actually a second derelict ship, hidden in plain sight. The structures built all around its sides and especially over its upended ring section had disguised it pretty well. But once it had been pointed out to her, she couldn't unsee it.

She had seen two starships, ships with enormous engines capable of carrying thousands of people from star to star. And she knew she had only seen parts of those ships, as both had been buried nose-down in the ground for centuries. She had to extrapolate the full size of them. But the massive ring sections that once had housed all of those people? She had seen the full size of those.

She had marveled at the scale of it, even seen from a distance across the rooftops of the city. Or from the long climb up staircase after staircase when she had gone inside of it.

But she still kind of worried that the real appreciation she should have been feeling, the real depths of awe and wonder, just weren't there.

Was she growing dead inside? At the age of eighteen? Was that happening to her?

But she really needn't have worried. Sure, she had endured another long night's travel, and again by foot, but this time through damp, chilly tunnels under the streets of the capital city and not over hot, humid grasslands. But this walk hadn't been just her and Kora, and with Kora unable to speak aloud lest she be overheard. This time, it had been with her newfound friend Tristan Carey and his old friend Dieter Bohm.

Tristan, like her father, was a student of Uche Okafo who was secretly learning the real history of their world and its people, not the official, Central Planning-approved version. His friend Dieter Bohm wasn't a student. He also wasn't the street urchin his slovenly clothing and stooped, hollow-bellied posture were meant to evoke. Lafayette wasn't quite sure just what he was yet. He turned out to be the very opposite of an orphan, with a mind-boggling number of siblings who kept turning up at opportune moments to help the three of them escape the clutches of Central Planning.

Were they traders like the caravan clans she had travelled over the grasslands with? Or were they more like smugglers? Or even some kind of ragtag rebellion, hiding under the city inside the sewer system and finding little ways to disrupt Central Planning whenever they could?

Lafayette wasn't quite sure. But she was getting the sense that "all of the above" might be the correct answer.

But, as new and wonderful as traveling with friends was, that wasn't what sparked the sense of wonder she had been afraid she had lost.

No, that happened after they had left the sewer tunnels behind, just squeezing through a narrow fissure in the bedrock that charted a zigzag course, ever deeper but always heading more easterly than anything.

They were passing under the wall on the eastern edge of the city. During that long night, the three of them had walked the entire length of the city. No wonder her feet were so tired. And her body generally. But also her mind. She needed sleep so badly.

But all of that exhaustion just left her when the fissure opened up into an immense cavern nestled among the hills east of the city walls. The cavern was shaped like a round flask, wider on the bottom but curving in to a narrow neck that led up through the rocky hillsides to the sky above.

The sight that waited there in the heart of that cavern was one that left her gaping, wide-eyed and wide-mouthed, stumbling over her own tired feet until she gave up walking entirely just to drink in the vision before her.

She felt like that kid again, the one who had had endless time to lie under the branches of her village tree and look up at the sky and imagine things.

But she had never imagined anything like this.

"That's your family's airship?" Tristan said before Lafayette could make her mouth do anything other than hang open. But he sounded as awestruck as Lafayette felt. Which, given that he had lived his entire life inside the capital city and had grown up around all of its everyday wonders, made Lafayette feel a bit less foolish.

"Indeed, it is," Dieter said. Smugly as always, but Lafayette found that this time, she didn't mind. Just this once, that smirking twist to his lips felt earned.

The cavern they were standing in was so large she couldn't make out the far wall, although the first gray light of dawn was trickling down from the open top of the cavern above. That light might not be able to penetrate the rocky corners of the space below, but it lit up the cavern's central feature like a spotlight.

It danced over the curved sides of that airship as it towered over them. It gleamed silver-bright off of the network of ropes that held that ship down. And it glowed softly through the belly of its form, making it seem almost like a living thing. Like a lighter-than-air whale ready to swim up into the clouds.

Lafayette knew it was nothing next to the two starships she had seen. But those had been relics from the past, when her ancestors had known how to do so many long since forgotten things.

This airship was something her contemporaries had built. It was something she could almost understand. She had certainly read about them in books that weren't quite as forbidden as the ones her father had kept that mentioned the starships. Airships were a part of her world, the world she shared with the people living around her.

She had read about them, sure. She had seen pictures. She had thought she had understood their size.

But clearly she had been wrong.

CHAPTER 2

From everything Tristan had told her about his oldest friend, Dieter Bohm was a street urchin, an orphan doing what he had to do to survive in the narrow streets and alleys of the capital city.

But from everything she had gathered herself in the few days she'd spent with him, she knew Dieter was so much more than that. The waif look was a put-on. She knew the strength he was hiding could only come from ready access to plenty of healthy food. Not to mention a safe place to get restful sleep at night. She had known too many people who didn't have access to either to believe it was true of him after she'd seen him move through the city swiftly and without tiring.

She had begun to suspect he was not as disinterested in knowledge of the bookish variety as he had led Tristan to believe throughout their childhood either. She had yet to catch him with a book in his hands, reading. And yet, she was sure he understood what she and Tristan talked about better than he let on to Tristan.

Still, there was a huge gap between being better read and better fed than he was pretending to be, and having access to something as wondrous as the airship she was, admittedly, still gaping at.

For one thing, when did he find the time to lead his little gang of street urchins in their spying missions and black market shenanigans? Because she knew if she had a ship like this, she'd be spending all her time flying it around if that was even a possibility.

"You fly this?" she asked Dieter when she could finally summon up the words.

Dieter looked down at her with a grin. His usually slicked back dark hair had fallen forward over his forehead, making his gaunt face look a little bit softer than usual, his cheeks a little rounder. Not that she hadn't realized his appearance was a carefully calibrated facade. She knew he put great effort into seeming like any other young street urchin, too small for anyone to bother with. But she knew the body that looked thin and weedy in his tattered clothes was actually all hard muscle. She had seen him running and climbing and fighting his way through the city.

Now she was noticing something else about him. That hard look to his face was just as false. The smirks and the sneers were as much an act as the starving street kid look. Underneath it all, he was just as capable of gentle feelings of wonder as she was.

But then he reached a hand up, ran it over that hair, and it was like that slicking back changed his whole face. The smirk was back, and the softness to his cheeks was gone.

"You doubted me," he said.

"No," Lafayette said.

But Tristan spoke at the same time. "Shouldn't we be getting on board?"

Lafayette looked at him, taking in the exhaustion making his normally pale, freckled skin look positively gray, especially against the red of his hair. Unlike her, he wasn't used to hours upon hours of walking. And that was chiefly what they'd been doing since long before the last day's dawn. That little nap they had gotten just before things had gotten dangerously bad hadn't really counted.

"My sisters—" Dieter started to say, looking around with a frown.

But he was interrupted by a voice behind them. "Have been waiting for quite a long time for you to arrive."

Lafayette pivoted, annoyed at herself for not noticing they were being sneaked up on. But then Kora hadn't noticed it either. And Kora, with her unique combination of dog instincts and the intelligence of a construct within her that had been designed to teach children all they needed to know, was always on high alert.

She was bristling now, or as much bristling as she could do when her entire middle section was robotic. It was just a little lifting of the red hair at the back of her neck, and a bushing out of her long, brush-like tail.

But Dieter made a soft noise at her, not a word that Lafayette understood, but whatever it was, Kora relaxed at once.

It wasn't just one woman who had sneaked up behind them. It was two, one with long, pink hair pulled into a topknot and the other with short hair dyed a shade of blue that was almost teal. But they were clearly Dieter's sisters. As much as everyone in the Bohm family went out of their way to craft a unique appearance—his younger siblings almost genderless urchins while his two older brothers could pass for any of the office workers who flocked to the very heart of the capital every morning to get to their various Central Planning jobs on time— Lafayette was starting to get an eye for the features underneath that they just couldn't hide. The telltale signs said they were all definitely siblings.

Hair aside, Lafayette would bet money that unlike Dieter's brothers Karlo and Till, who strived to look identical although they were not, these two actually were twins.

"We made the best time we could," Dieter said, not quite shooting a glance Tristan's way. But Tristan flushed with embarrassment all the same.

Lafayette wanted to assure him that he hadn't slowed them down all that much, but Dieter's pink-haired sister was already talking, so she remained silent.

"Everything is on board," she said even as she started herding them with gestures to keep walking towards the airship.

"Cold-weather gear," the blue-haired sister said, "fuel and food enough for twenty days. Ronja even put a games table in there in case you get bored. Because she's a softie."

"I'm the softie?" Ronja shot back even as her steps leading them to the airship never slowed. "Ivka is the one who spent half the night and called in a *lot* of favors acquiring the nutritional paste that Finley said you needed."

"Nutritional paste?" Dieter said with a puzzled frown.

"For Kora," Lafayette told him. But she was as gobsmacked as he was. "But how did Finley know?"

"Uche," Tristan put in. "Uche knew you needed it."

"And if Uche was asking around to find a source for it, Finley would've heard," Dieter said.

Lafayette didn't doubt that for a minute. Finley, young as she was, had struck Lafayette as highly competent at what she did. And being part of a trading or smuggling or whatever kind of family, knowing what people were looking for but couldn't find on their own was definitely part of what she did.

But still. "I didn't know he'd even started looking," Lafayette said.

"I understand she doesn't need much," Ivka said. "But it was just as easy to acquire in bulk. The three of you will run out of food long before she needs a resupply. Long, long before."

"Thanks," Lafayette said. But Ivka just waved it off, as if gratitude annoyed her.

She really was Dieter's sister.

They finally reached their destination: the open door in the side of the gondola that was tucked almost out of sight beneath the immensity of the balloon part of the airship. It looked almost ridiculously tiny compared to all of that air-filled metallic fabric.

Then she stepped inside, following Dieter and Ronja, and realized it wasn't just a matter of scale. It really was very tiny. To the right of the doorway was an area that was separated by thin walls and an opening with no door, an area so crowded with controls and panels and great, curving windows like bubbles of glass that two people could only just manage to stand in the space in the center of it. It would be far more comfortable for just one.

There was a narrow closet across from the doorway she was stepping in from. Or so Lafayette thought at first. Then she saw the toilet and the sink stacked on top of each other, and she realized what she was looking at was the world's tiniest bathroom. If you could even call it a bathroom when there was no bath, not even a shower.

The rest of the gondola interior was one open space. The curved windows ran down both sides and all across the back, and Lafayette realized from the way they bubbled out like they did, it was possible to lean into them to look more or less straight down. That would be important once they were up in the air, she was sure.

But calling that space "open" was probably not the best word. It was all one room, but that room was almost impossibly cluttered. Crates of supplies were stacked against all three walls, but not so high as to block the windows. There were also a number of huge bottles of water, and sacks that Lafayette guessed were filled with either that cold-weather clothing they had mentioned or bedding to be rolled out at night, or both.

Crammed into the center of it all, making the space between it and the crates just barely passable, was that games table. It was built from wood like any other table, but its surface was painted with an almost indecipherable overlay of various game boards. And every side of the table had its own drawer, presumably filled with the pieces to be used on those boards.

Luckily, with the pieces put away, the surface was flat and uncluttered. Perfect for spreading out books and journals. Which, for the foreseeable future, was going to be what filled all of Lafayette's and Tristan's waking hours.

Central Planning may have burned all of her father's books. And they may have burned all of Uche's too, and everything that Tristan had been hiding in his secret room behind the library at the university.

But they hadn't touched the memories Lafayette and Tristan had of everything they had read. Only, if they didn't write it all down, it really could be lost. No one else would ever know what had been destroyed. And Lafayette worried that with every passing day, another memory of something she had seen or read would fade away. She wouldn't even know it was gone.

She had to write it all down before that happened. And she knew Tristan felt exactly the same.

Lafayette set her bag of journals and writing utensils on that table then stretched out her back as well as she could in the tight space.

It must have been obvious how awkward that stretch was, because

Ronja gave her a smile that wasn't quite one of Dieter's smirks, but was definitely related to it.

"Don't worry. Once Ivka and I step out of here, it's like you'll have twice the space," she said.

"I really do appreciate this," Lafayette said. "I assume, like your brothers, you already know about my father—"

"We do," Ronja cut in. "Pardon my rudeness, but you all need to get airborne before the sun gets any higher in the sky."

Lafayette nodded, but Ronja had already turned her attention to Dieter. "You're sure you can handle this?"

"Because, again, I can stay and fly for you," Ivka put in.

"I've got it," Dieter said, his jaw tightening. Interesting how he didn't smirk at his sisters. His *older* sisters. Maybe that was the difference.

"Like you had it last winter festival," Ivka went on.

"That was more than a year ago, and this is different," Dieter said. "This is important. Now, kindly, get off my ship. And help me make way," he added with a little belated gentleness.

Ivka gave him a tight smile and a punch on the shoulder, then ducked out of the gondola.

But Ronja paused a moment, giving Dieter a more unreadable expression.

Dieter just said. "I know. And we will. I promise."

"I have your word on that," Ronja said gruffly. Then she pulled Dieter into a quick, tight hug before just as quickly pulling away, ducking her head so her face was out of sight of the others and following her sister out the door.

"We will what?" Tristan asked quietly. For which Lafayette was grateful. She had had the same question, but lacked the years of friendship that would actually make it askable. "Be careful?" he guessed when Dieter still said nothing.

"See each other again," Dieter said, his voice even more gruff with stifled emotion than his sisters.

Then he pulled the door shut, fastened the latches to hold it fast, and turned away from the two of them to stand before that array of controls.

"Just a little longer," Lafayette said to Tristan. "We get up into the sky, turn the nose to face north, and put the capital city far, far behind us. Then we can rest."

"Just a few more minutes of intense anxiety, and then we can rest," Tristan said with a dry scoff.

But, as it turned out, they couldn't have been more wrong.

CHAPTER 3

Things started out smoothly enough. Which, given Lafayette knew the top of the cavern was like a bottleneck, but one so narrow the airship barely had clearance around it to keep from scraping against all that rock, was impressive. On top of that, while looking down directly below them was possible with some careful leaning into the various bubble-shaped windows, there was no way to look up. Not unless all you were interested in seeing was the bottom of the airship balloon that spread far beyond the confines of the gondola in every direction.

Lafayette wasn't even sure how Dieter managed it. She didn't want to distract him with questions, but she did stay just out of his way in the space between the latched doorway and the accordion curtain of the toilet closet so she could watch everything that was going on.

She thought there was some sort of communication going on between him and his two sisters below. She had watched as they ran from post to post, releasing all the ropes that held their ship down in the center of that cavern. The airship had started rising at once, and Dieter had made constant adjustments to hold it steady until his sisters were done.

Then he kept looking down their way, even when they had shrunk down to the size of dots below them. He would lean forward over his controls and see *something* they were doing, then lean back to make another little adjustment to their steady elevator-like ascent.

She didn't know how they were communicating with each other, but she was sure it was happening. And—if these two were in charge of launching this airship on a regular basis—she thought the odds were good that looking different from each other wasn't the only reason these twins had brightly colored hair. It was just why they picked two different but equally bright colors.

Then, with a blinding suddenness, they were clear of the last of the rocky bottleneck. Lafayette was still blinking sun-dazzled tears from her eyes even as she felt the airship move beneath her. Dieter was changing their heading.

But then she heard a sharp hiss as he sucked a breath in between clenched teeth.

She wiped at her eyes, but she didn't need to hear his words to know what she was about to see.

"Company," was all he said, but so low it was almost to himself.

Then Tristan from the back of the gondola shouted towards the front. "Guys? I see five... no, six other airships."

Then he was standing just behind Lafayette, holding onto the walls although so far the movement of the airship had been surprisingly steady. He leaned close behind Lafayette's shoulder to look through the front windows. "More here. I think ten in all."

"I see them," was all Dieter said. He halted the turning motion of the airship, stopping when their nose faced not north but due east, towards the rising sun. The blinding rising sun.

Lafayette blinked then looked away, back at Tristan's worried face. "You've seen airships over the city before, right?" she asked him. "I haven't seen any since I got here a few days ago, but I've seen pictures in books. They carry cargo up to the mini-city on top of the pillar that's the crashed spaceship. Right?"

"Right," Tristan said, but she could tell he was hedging.

"Never this many," she guessed.

"Frankly, I can remember one single day when I saw two in the sky at the same time," he said. Then he looked away from the windows to pin her with those hazel eyes of his. "One time. When I was five."

"So this is about us," Lafayette said.

"Well," Dieter said in his most jocular tone, even as his hands never stopped moving from lever to lever, from control to control. He spared the two of them the briefest of glances over his shoulder to say, "I think it's about me."

Then he jammed the largest of the levers that was set into the floor of the cockpit as far forward as it would go. And Lafayette heard engines she hadn't even realized were there roaring to life. She clutched at Tristan to keep from falling into him from the sudden acceleration, but once they reached a steady speed, she let him go again.

"About you?" Lafayette asked.

"Well, my family," Dieter said with a shrug without looking back at them. "They know who I am by now, and they know I helped you get away from their clutches yesterday. I'm sure whatever intel they have on the Bohm family is a riot of deliberate falsifications. My father was a big believer in making sure all sorts of implausible rumors reached the ears of Central Planning, so any truth they discovered about us would be lost in a deluge of lies. But at the very least, they know we have access to five airships. And this is the largest of them."

"They're all over the city in a search pattern," Tristan said. "They don't know where you launch from."

"Well, they didn't," Dieter said. "I'm guessing that's about to change. Two of them for sure have spotted us. We'll have all twelve on our tail before breakfast time."

"But we can get away from them," Lafayette said. "This ship is top of the line. Right?"

Dieter gave her another of his brief glances, mostly so she could see that smirk again. "It's the top of *our* line. I assure you, Central Planning has far more resources than my little family of smugglers. We mostly get by with not being noticed in the first place."

"It's my fault," Tristan said, and at first Lafayette honestly didn't know what he was talking about. But then he went on. "I was too slow. We could've launched before sunrise if I had been just a little bit faster."

"You're on two nights running with no sleep," Lafayette reminded him.

"We all are," Tristan pointed out.

"We were all too slow, but it's not like it mattered," Dieter said. "It was a cloudless night with both moons full. This airship would've been almost easier to spot by night than it is now, with us aiming straight for the sun."

So that explained the due east course, then. Not only were they not letting on which direction they ultimately wanted to be heading, they were also using the blinding brightness of the sun itself for cover.

Although that was only going to last for so long. And some of the ships had spotted them already.

"If they're faster than us, what can we do?" Lafayette asked.

"Fly smarter," Dieter said. He didn't look back, but he didn't need to. That time, Lafayette could just hear the smirking grin in his voice.

"You're hoping they won't follow us out over the open water of the sea?" Tristan asked with a frown.

"The sea is a little further away than it looks like on maps," Dieter told him. "At top speed, it would still be dark again before we reached it."

"So what, then?" Tristan asked.

But Lafayette had a hunch even before Dieter pointed to something ahead of them and slightly to the left. A bank of clouds. Thick and white like fluffy cotton, but taller than any mountain.

"How can you see in there?" she asked in the tiniest of voices.

"Won't need to," he said. "The point is not to be seen. Those ships are going to have to slow down if they follow us in there. And since we're heading due east, the odds of one getting ahead of us and making an obstruction I'd have to see to dodge is pretty low."

"But not zero," Lafayette said.

"Well," Dieter said, that grin back in his voice. "What's the fun of zero risk?"

"We'll be okay," Tristan said. But Lafayette was fairly certain he was talking to himself and not to her.

Dieter kept the engines at full power, but their steady roar quickly faded into the background. It was almost like Lafayette wasn't hearing it anymore, although she knew it was still there. Like with smells that seemed strong at first but at some point you just stopped smelling them, even though they were still there.

Lafayette realized she was feeling dizzy, then realized that was because she was holding her breath. Only after taking a breath did she become aware of just how tense her entire body was. Her jaw was tight, her shoulders were scrunched up tight, her hands were in fists. It was like she was bracing for a blow that wasn't coming. And it kept on not coming.

"Diet," Tristan said suddenly. "You hungry?"

"I'm so hungry I could eat Kora," he said, but with fondness in his voice. "Well, I'd pick out her metal bits. After which, I'm not sure there'd be much left. Do you want to dig into what Ronja and Ivka packed for us?"

"Speaking of Kora," Lafayette said as she followed Tristan into the back of the gondola. She wanted to find that crate of nutritional paste, as she was sure Kora was hungrier than any of them, if disinclined to complain. But for a moment, Lafayette was just struck with the image of twelve silvery dots in the blue sky behind them.

"They look so far away," she said softly.

"They might not be putting on their own top speed," Tristan said. "If they think they can run longer than us, maybe they don't need to. They'll just wait until we run out of fuel and go down, and then they'll pick us up."

"Ronja said we had enough for twenty days," Lafayette said.

"They don't know that," Tristan said. Then he started examining the neatly printed labels on the crates below the nearest window.

Lafayette chewed at her lip. Central Planning might, indeed, not know how prepared they were to keep flying.

But then again, they might.

And even if they didn't, they never did anything without a carefully thought-through plan.

It was, after all, half of their name.

"This one's Kora's," Tristan told her, pulling her out of her reverie. She took the crate from him with a mumble of thanks, then opened the lid to pull out one of the unlabeled tubes made of soft metal. A quick look around showed her a detail she had missed before: the wall that didn't have windows, the one that divided the toilet closet from the rest of the room, also had crates stacked against it, but they went no higher than the other stacks. But while the others stopped at the bottom of the windows, these stopped at the bottom of a row of cabinets.

Something about those cabinets just screamed "galley," although she couldn't see any of their contents until she started opening doors. But that was indeed what they were. The largest of the cabinets held more wonders that Lafayette had only read about but never seen: an electric cooker for soups or porridge, an electric skillet for frying things, and an electric kettle for beverages. But the next one over held stacks of plates, bowls, and cups.

Lafayette took down one of the bowls, then twisted the cap off the tube of nutritional paste. She squeezed what she knew was a double portion into the bowl, then set it down on the floor between Kora's paws.

Kora had been sitting up but in a half-doze, her eyes blinking closed more than open. But she perked up at the scent of the grayish ooze that was her food, looking up at Lafayette with bright, happy eyes even as her tail swished the floor behind her clean.

"You're awfully quiet," Lafayette said.

"Just tired," Kora said. Given that her human voice came from the construct built into her torso, she could easily speak and eat at the same time. But it was still unsettling to watch.

"Yeah, I think we all are," Lafayette said.

Tristan banged around in the galley cabinets briefly, then took out the electric kettle and filled it from one of the water bottles before plugging it into an outlet that Dieter's sisters had carefully left exposed when they'd been stacking all those crates.

"I found oatmeal that just needs hot water to become food, and I stopped digging around," Tristan said. He almost sounded apologetic, like she or Dieter had been expecting him to whip up a home-cooked meal of bacon and eggs or something.

"Oatmeal sounds perfect right now," she assured him. She toyed with adding on her second thought—that with all the anxiety this day was steeped with, the idea of eating anything more challenging for her stomach than cereal was almost repellent—but opted not to.

He already knew they were all anxious. No one needed to be saying it out loud.

The kettle whistled, a surprisingly cheerful sound, loud even against the background of the droning of the engines. Tristan shut it off with a snap of the switch, then filled each of the three containers he had arranged on the games table. After setting the kettle aside, he stirred the first of the containers thoroughly and then handed it to Lafayette with a tired sort of smile, then picked up the second, stirring it even as he carried it up to Dieter in the cockpit.

Lafayette spooned a mouthful of oatmeal into her mouth and realized too late that it was still a bit on the hot side. But she sucked in a few cooling breaths as she watched Kora lick the already thoroughly clean bowl just a little more thoroughly clean.

"Do you want some more?" Lafayette asked around her mouthful of hot oatmeal.

"No," Kora said, but regretfully. "This body can only process so much at once. In fact, I think for the next meal we should go back to the normal amount." While the construct said all that, the dog's tongue never stopped lapping at the bowl.

"Okay," Lafayette said, her words still muffled by the food. "How about some water?"

"Yes, please," Kora said, and Lafayette set her oatmeal aside to bring the slightly slimy bowl over to the water bottle to fill it.

She set the bowl down and smothered a laugh at how eagerly Kora devoured its contents. But as she reached for her now cooler oatmeal, she happened to glance up out of those windows again.

And saw the dots of pursuing ships were closer now. A lot closer. They weren't dots anymore. No, the dots now were the dark outlines of people she could just make out moving around inside the gondolas of those ships.

"Dieter?" she called nervously.

"It's okay," Tristan said as he slipped past her to reach for his still unstirred oatmeal. "He knows. But we're nearly there."

As if that had been some kind of cue, Lafayette saw white wisps blowing past the windows. Those wisps of cloud grew denser, but sporadically, like a stutter of white. Then one thicker patch coated the exterior of all the windows in fat droplets of water. All of those droplets caught the light from the sun in dazzling brightness for the briefest of moments as they flew through another thin patch.

And then, with a suddenness that felt kind of final, everything outside the gondola became an impenetrable world of gray. Droplets were always forming outside the windows, but then streaking away towards the back of the ship, only to be replaced with yet more droplets.

"How big is the cloud?" Lafayette wondered.

"Let's just hope it's big enough," Tristan said.

They both ate their oatmeal in silence, not really tasting it. But their bodies needed the fuel.

And sleep. But it was going to be hours yet before that would even be thinkable.

CHAPTER 4

I n Lafayette's mind, being inside that cloud was supposed to feel like safety. And yet, once they were in it and its heavy, wet darkness obscured the view in every possible direction, she just felt trapped.

Worse, she couldn't even tell if Dieter's plan was working. If she couldn't see the Central Planning dirigibles, how could she tell if they were still hot on their tail, or if they were falling behind?

Lafayette tasted copper in her mouth and realized she had bitten deeply enough into her lip to draw blood. Her entire body was so tightly clenched it actually hurt. She took a deep breath, then another and another. She slowly found her way back to a calmer state.

Then, with far more abruptness than entering the cloud had seemed, they burst out the far side. They were in the full sun once more, a sun higher and brighter in the sky than when she'd last seen it. The droplets that still clung stubbornly to the windows sparkled like gemstones, but Lafayette ignored them to stare past them. Back to the cloud they had just been hiding in.

She counted her breaths, as if that measure of time could possibly mean something. One breath. Two. Deep, slow breaths, even as she realized her hands were in fists again. Like she was preparing for a fight.

At fourteen breaths, the first of the Central Planning airships broke free from the cloud. At sixteen breaths, it was joined by two more.

"Do they see us?" Tristan said in a whisper. As if the people on those ships behind them could possibly overhear.

"We gained some ground, didn't we?" she found herself whispering back. "They were closer to us when we went into the cloud."

"Maybe?" Tristan said, although his tone was leaning more towards a no.

"We're heading into another cloud," Dieter called back to them. "If we're lucky, they won't spot us before we're out of their sight again."

Tristan moved closer to the back window as if hoping to see inside the gondolas of the pursuing ships, to tell if they could see Dieter's airship as easily as they had spotted the Central Planning ships.

But Lafayette turned the other way, moving as close as she dared behind Dieter, not wanting to get in the way of any lever or control he might need to reach in a hurry. The cloud bank he was heading for now was a little south of due east. It was also massive, whiter and fuller than the last cloud had been. Would the glittering of the sunlight on the droplets in that cloud be enough to mask the shining of the airship exterior from view?

She tried to make a mental image of the relative positions of their ship, the pursuing ships, the cloud and the sun, but it was a lot to juggle on so little sleep. Before she had more than a rough outline in her mind, they were once more flying through the dense fog of the cloud's interior, and the question became moot.

"Can we keep doing this all day?" she asked the moment she saw Dieter relax at the controls.

"If the clouds keep up," he said. "More clouds would be nice."

"Can *you* keep doing this all day?" Tristan asked pointedly as he joined Lafayette in the cockpit doorway.

"Well, I have to, don't I?" Dieter said with a humorless laugh. "Look, I fully intend to teach the two of you how to fly this machine. Because I have to sleep sometime. Being at the mercy of the winds, there is no scenario where we can fly without someone at the controls."

"Is there a manual I can study?" Tristan asked, peering all around the interior of the cockpit.

"Not that you can read," Dieter said, although even as he said it he pulled something out of a cubby over his side of the doorway where Lafayette and Tristan stood. It wasn't really a book. It wasn't even a pamphlet. It was just a stack of loose pages held together with brass fasteners. Everything in it had been written by hand, but the ink had faded and the pages themselves were smudged from the oils of many people's fingers.

Also, it wasn't in any language Lafayette could read. They weren't the letters of the modern world, or the letters their ancestors had used on board their spaceships. More than that, as much as those two languages had felt so different when she'd first tried learning the older language, she had quickly realized just how related they were. The shapes of the letters had changed over time, but they, fundamentally, had the same intentionality. They represented the same sounds.

But this? This looked like so many dots and scratches to her eyes. And she couldn't even discern a flow of left to right or up to down or anything that told her what order anything was meant to be read in. Had the person writing this been just that sloppy? Or was the language itself this disorganized?

Lafayette turned the pages of the little book, examining each page in turn as if something somewhere might spark an insight. But Tristan only gave it a single glance, blanched, then turned his attention to the controls themselves that clustered around the spot where Dieter stood.

"It's a basic machine," he said. "Everything is arranged to require the least amount of effort from you. It's got to be understandable."

"Oh, you'll pick it up in no time, I have no doubt," Dieter said. "But teaching is going to have to wait until we're free of our pursuers."

And who knew how long that would take? Lafayette was thinking it, but she didn't say it. She was pretty sure they were all thinking it.

"Coffee?" Tristan said at last.

"Please," Dieter said, leaning forward to peer up through the bubble of window, like he was trying to pinpoint the sun through the dense mass of cloud.

"I'll quietly observe, shall I?" Kora offered. "I don't take up much space. But I'm curious how this ship works."

"Be my guest," Dieter said, even moving a little to his left so that Kora could slide most of the way into the cockpit to have a better view.

Lafayette clutched the loose pages in her hand and looked at all of those controls one last time. Even if she decoded the book and understood the writing, none of the controls themselves were labelled at all.

She didn't think learning how to fly the ship was going to be anywhere near as easy as Dieter and Tristan were trying to make it seem.

She brought the pages with her to the back of the gondola and put them next to her bag with her writing supplies and the tablet they had stolen from the spaceship hidden in the heart of the capital city what felt like an eternity ago.

"Did you want coffee, or are you going to try to get some sleep?" Tristan asked as he turned from the kettle he had just switched on to the cabinet where the mugs sat neatly in a row. He took down two mugs before throwing her a questioning look, so she knew which option he was taking.

"Coffee," she said, although she had never wanted anything less in her life.

He just nodded, took down a third mug, then began spooning brownish crystals from a jar into each.

Lafayette had rarely had coffee before. In the village where she had grown up, it had been a precious commodity only available sporadically. Bandits on the roads were a plague on the traders, and the trading clans rich enough to hire the security necessary to carry such valuable goods tended not to waste their time with places the size of her hometown.

But that coffee had always been in the form of roasted beans that had to be ground up and put in some kind of filter. So, Lafayette was a little surprised to see Tristan just pour boiling water into each of the mugs and stir them up before handing the mugs around.

It was a little like the freeze-dried rations that Lafayette had gotten used to eating when traveling with her father. Those had also involved adding hot water to the contents. The results had never quite been satisfying, but they had kept hunger at bay.

Lafayette blew the steam from the surface of her mug and then took a sniff. It certainly smelled the way she remembered coffee was supposed to smell.

Alas, the taste was too much like the taste of all of that freeze-dried food. It did the job of delivering caffeine, but it didn't fuss with little details like flavor.

Or even texture. Particularly the last swallow, which was distinctly gritty.

She was just choking that last bit down when the gray fog outside the windows lightened to a whiter shade of gray, then broke into wisps before trailing away behind them.

Then Lafayette was counting her breaths again. She got to twenty-four this time before the first of their pursuers burst out of the cloud bank behind them. And she got to forty before the second emerged.

"They're losing contact with each other," Tristan said. "That's a good thing, right?"

"It only takes one to board us," Dieter said over his shoulder. "But no worries. I'll have us under cover again in just a moment."

"This is amazing, Lafayette," Kora said with doggy enthusiasm. "I'm learning so much up here!"

"It's a shame nothing is fitted to work with dog paws," Dieter said with a laugh. "Still, she's going to be an able teacher's assistant when the time comes."

Lafayette made a murmur of noise that she hoped sounded supportive, but she couldn't take her eyes off of the view through the back window. She could see six airships now, but where were the others? In the cloud behind them still? Or did they turn back, or get hopelessly lost?

She wanted to believe any or all of those things. But the niggling worry in the back of her mind still insisted on positing that they could just as likely be ahead of their position. Waiting. Laying a trap.

She still only saw six behind them when Dieter flew them into yet another mass of cloud.

Was this how the day was going to go? Slowly losing pursuers in twos or threes as they flew from cloud to cloud?

And there was absolutely nothing she could do but wait and see. That was the worst part for her.

She looked down at the corner of the stolen tablet just visible where the flap of her bag lay open on the tabletop. She didn't understand most of what she had seen on the spaceship she had explored while trying to free her father from the brig he had gotten himself trapped in. And her time in the ship at the heart of the capital had been beyond fleeting. But still, she had seen enough to know.

Her ancestors had ways of dealing with this sort of thing. They had ways of knowing where things were. And if she could just get enough time to study them properly, she could master those technologies herself.

The tablet wasn't any kind of textbook or manual. It was just the private diary of a young engineer. But it was a place to start.

If only she could get enough time.

Lafayette climbed up onto the last row of storage crates so she could sit facing the back window, arms wrapped around her drawn-up knees, and waited for the cloud they were in to pass away behind them. Counting breaths and counting airships. It was all she could do for now.

CHAPTER 5

As the day progressed, the clouds became fewer and farther between. But while the number of breaths it took until the ships appeared increased to nearly a hundred, the number of ships stayed consistently at six.

"Maybe we should change our heading while we're in a cloud?" Tristan said at some point in the middle of the afternoon. Lafayette just sat where she had been all day, staring glassy-eyed out the back window. But she listened. She listened intently for what Dieter would say.

"Not north, obviously," Tristan went on when Dieter said nothing. "But a little south? Just to throw them off?"

"Look, two things," Dieter said, sounding every bit as exhausted as Lafayette felt. "We'd have to burn fuel we're going to want later if we do that."

"Aren't we doing the same thing just going east?" Tristan asked. Which was Lafayette's question too at first. But even before Dieter spoke again, she brought up a mental map, not of a flat surface like the maps her father had drawn that they were using their collective memories of as reference, but of a globe. Because the world was mostly spherical. And where they were going was north, but not all the way north.

"It's not the most direct way, but it's not that far off the optimal route," Dieter said even as Lafayette came to the same conclusion. "But there's another reason to head due east."

"No settlements?" Tristan guessed. Because most of the population of her world lay north, south and west of the capital city. Everything to the east was an unforgiving rocky wasteland, completely unsuitable for farming. At least, until you reached…

"The ocean," Dieter said as if completing her thought. "We're nearly there. It's the best place to lose them for sure. There's always the possibility of spies on the ground who could see our heading and report us to Central Planning. But no one sails out of sight of shore on the ocean."

"There are rumors of an island prison," Tristan said.

Dieter said nothing. But Lafayette didn't have to turn her head to know just how skeptical a look he was giving Tristan right now. It was all too apparent in the nervous throat-clearing sound Tristan made before he ducked back out of the cockpit again.

The sky became cloudless not long after that conversation, and Lafayette, who had been drifting in and out of a sleep she didn't want to have whenever the windows were grayed out by clouds, now had a couple of uninterrupted hours of staring unblinkingly at the six dots that were still in pursuit of their airship.

They were very far behind now. But as she stared at them, they were getting bigger. Closer. And yet, their number stayed at six.

Then, without any warning from Dieter, they were plunged into another bank of clouds. This one seemed darker than any of the others, although given that the sun was setting far behind them, that might have just been because of the time of day.

But it also lasted longer than the others. By the time they burst through on the other side, the sun was entirely gone below the horizon. Although the last of its reddish glow was visible still, dancing on the water below.

The water. So much water. Lafayette, who had been more asleep than awake by that point, was suddenly completely alert. She shifted from sitting on her butt to perching on her hands and knees, pressing her forehead to the surprisingly chilly glass of the window.

She scanned the entire world below her, but there wasn't a hint of rock or ground anywhere. There was nothing but water, more water than she had ever seen before in her life. And she could see it moving, the tops of the waves catching the last of the sun in little sparkles that were fading away even as she gazed at them.

"Have you ever seen anything like this?" Tristan asked, suddenly close by her side, also with his face pressed close to the glass.

And Lafayette remembered that as much as he had grown up in the capital city and took for granted things like trams crisscrossing the skies over the city and the very airship they were traveling on now, he had never strayed outside of those walls once in his entire life.

In a way, she took for granted just as many marvelous things that he did. They were just of a different variety.

"I've seen a few rivers," she said. "One was moving so fast the water was all white foam crashing over rocks until it fell over a cliff to a pool below. I watched a fallen tree branch float over those falls. It got churned under in that pool, and it never came back up again. That was loud and intense."

She only had to close her eyes to summon back that memory even now. It was one of the first things she had seen since leaving the crater behind where she had lost her father. When her relationship with Kora and the construct inside of her had still felt so new.

"But this?" Lafayette said, and turned to look Tristan full in the eye and share an ecstatic grin with him. "This is amazing. I wonder if it's loud? If we're closer to it?"

"It has to be," Tristan said. "You know, I've seen it on maps my whole life. I knew it was big. But this just makes that sound like too small a word. Doesn't it?"

"Let's look out the front," Lafayette said, scrambling down from her perch to rush to the cockpit.

"No sign of pursuit?" Dieter asked, and Lafayette felt her face flush in acute embarrassment. Of course he'd think she was rushing up here to tell him something important, not just to sightsee.

And yet, wasn't the sight of it all moving to him as much as her?

"It's hard to tell," she said. "The sun is down. There's a little light on the water, but the sky is dark. Especially where that cloud bank is."

"That's all right," he said as if he had expected that to be her answer. "I'm going to bring us down a bit, but I'm keeping her locked due east until morning. Then, when we can be sure we're alone out here, I'll turn her north."

"A sensible plan," Lafayette said, even as she tried to crane her neck to look past him without being obvious about it.

But clearly she failed, as he chuckled, if equal parts amused and exhausted.

"Sorry, I *do* remember the first time I flew over the ocean. I was three or so. It's kind of a formative memory. But I've been out here a lot since then," he said.

"Why?" Lafayette asked. Because, as much as she knew his family traded on the black markets, there was literally nothing out here but water.

"Sometimes an airship needs to disappear for a while," he said, gesturing with his hands palms-up at the water and sky around them. "This is a great place to do that."

"It's why we came this way," Lafayette said. "You've done this before, so you knew it would work."

"I knew it would *probably* work," he amended. "But it was the best plan, yes."

"Although I'm not sure if her dog eyes are better than my human ones, Kora agrees there is no sign of pursuit behind us," Tristan said as he crowded up behind Lafayette. "Ready to teach me enough about this ship to let you get some kind of nap?"

"Are *you* up for it?" Dieter asked, staring significantly at the dark smudges under Tristan's eyes.

"Hey," Tristan said, rubbing at his eyes self-consciously. "You know my pale skin makes everything look worse than it is. I caught a couple of winks while we were locked in clouds. That's far more than you've had. You need a break."

"We need you to have a break," Lafayette added. "Who knows what tomorrow will require of you?"

"Fair enough," Dieter said. "It's not that complicated, really."

Then he started pointing at levers and knobs and brass wheels he spun by hand, and as much as Lafayette knew he was explaining it all in the simplest terms he could, it all kept devolving into walls of sound in her ears. She could follow the cadence of his speech, and she nodded in all the right places when his voice rose to a questioning intonation. But she couldn't make the sounds he was uttering form into words in her mind that made sense to her. At all.

It was like he kept barking at her like Kora used to before she had become half-robot. She knew something was being communicated to her. She just couldn't make it make sense.

"Lafayette?" Tristan said, not for the first time, and Lafayette realized she had dozed off while still standing up, just sort of leaning against the doorway.

"Sorry," she said, snapping to attention. "What did I miss?"

"All of it, I think," Dieter said with a smirk.

"Sorry," she said again, but Dieter just waved her words away.

"It's okay," Tristan said. "I think I've got it. At least, enough to keep us going the way we're going. I'll wake you up if anything changes. But, please, get some shuteye."

"I'll be here to assist," Kora said primly, and Lafayette saw that at some point Dieter had made a little nest for her out of one of the blankets from the storage crates. She even had a water bowl there, nestled against a cluster of wrapped wires that ran from the bottom of the control panel above to a hole set where the wall of the gondola met the floor.

"You both should get some sleep," Tristan said. "Kora and I have this."

Lafayette wanted to argue, but she simply didn't have the energy. But she couldn't bring herself to give up either. She just ended up in no fixed state, wavering in the doorway, still semi-leaning on the frame.

"You were vigilant all day, watching out the back windows," Tristan told her as he took her by the shoulders to get her moving towards the back of the gondola.

"I was fighting to stay awake," Lafayette said. Then had to add, "And I was losing. A lot."

"I surrendered," he told her. "You didn't see me tucked up inside my bedroll for most of the afternoon?"

"No," Lafayette said. She was pretty sure she had heard him talking for at least part of the afternoon. But her memories of the entire day were flickers of bright sunlight overwhelmed by longer chunks of the dark gray of clouds pressing in all around her. She couldn't be sure of anything.

"Well, I did," Tristan assured her. "Now it's your turn. When you're up again, we'll have another go at Dieter explaining the ship to you. I think it will stick, once you're a little more awake."

"I've never needed to be told how to do anything twice before," she admitted. And hated the tight feeling in her throat that made those words so very hard to say.

"I don't think this counts," Tristan said amiably. "You didn't really hear anything the first time. It doesn't count."

Lafayette didn't see it that way, but she just nodded numbly and then stumbled to the back of the gondola.

And straight into Dieter, who was in the process of slipping off his shoes.

"Sorry," she said, for what she knew was far from the last time.

"Can you believe my whole family used to travel in this thing?" Dieter said. "Of course, that was back when there were only five of us kids plus my parents."

"No, I don't believe it," Lafayette said.

"There's more room without the crates," he said even as he climbed into the bedroll that he had spread out on the floor under the gaming table. Because that was the only bit of floor space large enough to allow room for his lanky frame.

No wonder Lafayette hadn't seen Tristan napping. He would've been out of sight from her up on the crates.

Lafayette slipped out of her shoes, then found her own bedroll stacked with Tristan's neatly folded one in an open crate. The exterior had a rough, leathery texture to it, probably designed to be waterproof. Not really needed inside the gondola, but a nice feature if one was traveling the roads as Lafayette had done for so many days in the not too distant past.

But once she had crawled inside it, Lafayette found the interior was lined with a soft fur, both thick and warm. Not as thick as a mattress, but still better than lying on the metal floor of the gondola without it would be. Lafayette curled up inside the bag, knees close to her nose, head totally covered by the layers of fur and leather.

It shut out most of the engine noise. As much as she had gotten used to the ever-present roar and clatter, the relative silence inside her bedroll was bliss on her throbbing ears.

She was asleep before she'd counted a single breath.

CHAPTER 6

afayette woke to the familiar sensation of Kora licking all over her face. She might have the mind of an adult schoolteacher speaking through her midsection these days, but the construct and the dog worked in tandem to control the being called Kora. Sometimes, the doggy half's urges were too strong for the schoolteacher half to overcome.

"Sorry," Kora said even as that dog tongue kept lapping at her face. "Tristan wanted me to wake you up. I can't seem to not do it this way."

"It's fine," Lafayette said, throwing her arms around the dog and burying her face in the reddish fur of her warm neck. "I think your dog half is low on cuddles. That's my fault."

"Well," Kora said primly. "That *should* be understandable. Given the sequence of events."

"Try explaining that to a dog, though," Lafayette said. She gave Kora one last good scratch around the ears, then emerged from the bedroll and felt around in the relative darkness under the table for her shoes.

It was light out, but it was still a dim sort of light. Dawn, then, or maybe just a bit earlier.

Lafayette crawled out from under the table and made a half-hearted attempt at folding her bedroll before stuffing it back into the crate with the others. Then she shuffled to the cockpit, fluffing her sleep-flattened buns back to their proper, perfectly spherical poufs.

"Look at that," Dieter said, spreading his hands expansively at the view out of all three windows. He looked for all the world like he'd slept for days and was fully recharged now, ready for anything.

Lafayette doubted she looked so good herself. She certainly didn't feel anything like fully recharged. But, one way or another, she was determined to be ready for anything the day might bring.

But then she took in the view that Dieter was showing her. And then she rushed to the back window to do the same from that vantage point.

"They're gone," Lafayette said, scanning the same views of sea and sky she'd already scanned ten times already. But she couldn't quite bring herself to believe it.

"We'll keep a sharp eye out, of course, but yes," Dieter said with a wide grin. "I do believe they've gone."

"We're turning the ship northward now," Tristan told her with a grin of his own. "Nothing between us and our destination but water."

"And ice," Dieter reminded him. "When we get closer, it's nothing but ice."

"How long until we get there?" Lafayette asked.

"At our current speed? Five days," Dieter said, with a waffling hand gesture that seemed to add a "give or take" to that estimate.

"Five days there, plus the one we've already flown," Lafayette said. "So six days to get back again."

"We could maybe do it in five with the more direct route, but six is the safer bet, yes," Dieter said.

"And your sisters gave us fuel enough for twenty days. So that only leaves us…" Her tired mind was still fighting the strain of math, even basic arithmetic, but she held up a hand to keep the others from jumping in before she got there. "Eight days to search?"

"You have a spot marked on the map," Dieter said.

"It's a best guess," Tristan said. "An approximation."

"A starting point," Lafayette said. "It might take time—" But she broke off, shaking her head at her own word choices. "No, it *will* take more time than that to find it. I doubt it will be so obvious as the ship in the center of the capital city."

"Oh, the ship no one sees even though it's right there?" Tristan said with a wry twist of his mouth.

"If you knew what you were looking for, it was a bit more obvious," Lafayette said. "But the ship my father found was covered in jungle. *Covered.* He spent years practically right on top of it before he found it."

"We don't have years," Dieter said. "We have eight days. And there's no point in arguing about it. There's nothing to be done. After eight days, we'll have to turn back. Not to the capital city, because that's insane, but to one of my family's hidden compounds."

"We can refuel and come back?" Tristan said hopefully.

But the look on Dieter's face was not encouraging. "It really depends on what we find when we get to your spot on the map," he said. "If we find nothing, if it feels like a fool's errand, it's going to be very hard to convince my older siblings to give us a second shot at it. Fuel is expensive. My family does well as traders, but our coffers are far from bottomless. And even our kind of low-level acts of rebellion are costly. I know my siblings. They're going to pick the reliable results of continuing their form of rebellion over a second shot at finding something that might not be there anymore."

"We'll find something," Lafayette said. "We know better than even my father did what to be on the lookout for. And we have Kora with us. That's a huge advantage."

"If you say so," Dieter said. "She's certainly helped bring Tristan's flying skills up from nonexistent to merely abysmal."

"Hey," Tristan objected. But half-heartedly.

"You've been flying for a grand total of eight hours now," Dieter said. "In a straight line, in calm weather."

"Which was enough for you to get some sleep," Lafayette put in.

"I'm not complaining," Dieter said. "I'm just pointing out the facts. And the next fact on my list is that you still need to be trained up. Tristan and me doing twelve hours on and twelve hours off is going to burn us out long before we reach our goal. We need you in the rotation."

"Right," Lafayette said, trying hard to ignore the way her stomach had twisted into a tight knot and then sunk down low in cowering misery.

But it must've shown on her face anyway, because the sudden look of sympathy on Tristan's face was so intense it made her want to run away from all of them. A shame the gondola was so very small.

"Listen, you've been maintaining Kora since your dad fixed her up like this, right?" he said, running a hand over Kora's metallic torso. "And you tap your way through the controls on that electronic tablet like you were born doing it. Flying this ship? It's nothing like that technology at all."

"This ship is really basic," Dieter agreed with a solemn nod.

"Right," Tristan said, relieved at the unexpected backup.

But then Dieter had to ruin it by adding, "But the weather conditions you have to adapt to? The warning signs and how to respond to them? That's a whole other story. Mechanical knowledge of the airship is only the first thing to master."

"That's what you're here for, Diets," Tristan reminded him. "With your lifetime of experience with the weather and all."

"Okay," Lafayette said, taking a deep breath as she looked over all the controls arrayed throughout the tiny cockpit. "Take me through it again."

"As much as I could maybe use a refresher, I think I need sleep a little bit more," Tristan said, ducking out of the space to make room for Lafayette. "Eight hours in a row? Sounds divine."

"Ready?" Dieter asked her.

"One minute," she said, and ducked into the back to lunge at her bag and pull out a blank journal and a pen. She stepped back into the cockpit, turned to the first blank page and quickly but neatly recorded the date and time.

"Ready," Lafayette said with her most determined nod, and stood with pen poised.

So, Dieter went through it all again. And Lafayette found it actually made sense this time. Maybe it was the physical action of writing it all down, drawing her own diagrams of the controls and what they did to the outside of the airship, labeling the parts. That process of committing everything to paper helped her get things straight inside her own head. It always had.

But more likely, it was just that solid block of uninterrupted sleep. A few more of those, and she just might start feeling human again.

"And that's really all there is to it," Dieter finished with a shrug even as Lafayette raced to get down the last few details he had shared with her. "So why don't you go ahead and turn our nose northward."

"What, me?" she said, her pen jittering sloppily across the page. She frowned at the scrawl of ink then blinked up at Dieter.

"I think it should be you," he said. There was something in his voice that she had never heard there before. It was sincere emotion, no smirks or sarcastic angling of an eyebrow or anything.

Lafayette thought of her father, trapped somewhere up in space. He must've passed over this very ocean countless times since she had seen him last. Was the airship large enough for him to see from orbit? It was certainly large enough to make it pointless for Lafayette to try to gaze up past it, to hunt for the streak of light in the sky that marked her father's passing.

She closed the journal, tucked it in the large pocket at the back of her vest, and slid the pen into her breast pocket. Then she stepped forward and put her hands on those controls.

The brass was still warm from the sun or from Dieter's hands. It was hard to be sure which.

She checked all the gauges that he had just explained to her, remembering what she needed to see before she attempted to maneuver the ungainly ship. But the wind remained calm, the temperature of the air inside the balloon that kept them afloat in the sky neither too high nor too low. She put her hand on the wheel and turned it steadily until their heading shifted from due east to due north. Then she stopped and checked all the gauges again.

"See? Easy peasy," Dieter said. He was smirking, but Lafayette didn't mind. It felt like he was smirking at the universe at large and not at her. Like they were both getting away with something in this moment, taking this airship to find a location no human had seen in countless generations.

It had to still be there. It just had to.

Dieter left her in charge of the controls for most of the day, so she guessed that was her shift now. He set up a low, three-legged stool in the space between the hatch and the toilet closet and sat there, arms crossed, sometimes dozing and sometimes not. It was hard to tell. More than once, when she was sure he was deeply asleep, he'd draw her attention to something she should be watching more closely. And yet after she'd checked the gauge or scanned the horizon ahead, she'd look back to answer him and see his eyes still completely shut.

Dieter had her step out of the cockpit at two in the afternoon, pushing a barely awake Tristan into her place. Kora trotted after, turning around and around before getting comfortable in her nest among the controls.

"I'll stay with Tristan until you're rested," she said to Dieter. "Please do get some sleep. Real sleep."

"We need you on the night shift," Tristan said with an apologetic wince.

"I'll stay awake until then too," Lafayette promised. "The three of us should be able to handle almost anything."

"But we won't hesitate to wake you if we need you," Tristan added.

"You guys are acting like I'm going to argue with you," Dieter said with a shake of his head. Then he went into the back of the gondola, pulled out his bedroll, and curled up under the game table.

"I should get to work on my journal," Lafayette said. "I feel like I'm forgetting things already."

"Once you start writing, it will come back to you," Tristan said.

Lafayette certainly hoped that was true. The image of all her father's books, of all the books that Uche and Tristan had been hiding in the capital city, all burning together in an enormous pyre, haunted her still. She could hear the crackling of the flames. She could smell the paper as it turned to ash.

"We know there's a ship in the north," Tristan said as he rubbed a bit of moisture off of one of the brass controls with the side of his thumb. "And after seeing that ship for myself, not just the size of it but the complete solidness of it, and from what you described of that ship in the jungle, it just has to still be there, right? I mean, both of those ships fell down to the surface and left craters so huge the one that formed the capital city is almost too big to see, right? But those ships were still intact. So this one must be too."

"My father certainly thought so," Lafayette said. "If it was true for two of those ships, it must be for all five."

"Can you imagine?" Tristan said wistfully. "Once upon a time, our ancestors knew how to build things that could not only cross the stars to get here, but could survive such a catastrophic impact. And if we could only get time enough to study one, maybe we could learn how to do all that all over again."

"To travel across the stars?" Lafayette said. She'd honestly never contemplated such a thought before. The way her father talked about those ships, they were always things of the remote past. Not of the present, and certainly not of the future. Lafayette had thought of them the same way, as things to be studied and recorded in journals. She and her father had tinkered with some of the smaller technology, like figuring out how tablets worked, but she didn't think even he had ever considered taking one of the ships up into space.

But that was just what he had done, however inadvertently. And now all Lafayette had been thinking ever since was how she had to get him back. She had to get him off his spaceship and back down on the surface where he was safe. Where he'd be with her.

Only, what if more was possible?

What if she was facing a future that might be even bigger than her last seemingly impossible dream of attending the university in the capital city?

What would she do if traveling the stars were a possibility for her? Could she strive for it?

Or would this just be one more hope to be dashed by cold reality?

Lafayette shook the thought away and turned her attention to the journal in her hands, waiting to be filled with all she remembered of her parents' life's work. But it kept niggling at her, in the back of her mind, even as her hand raced across page after page.

What if she could leave this whole world behind and find a new one?

CHAPTER 7

The next five days, flying day and night northward-bound in the cramped gondola under the massive balloon of the airship, were the strangest in Lafayette's life. And given the twists and turns her life had taken so far, that was saying something.

It wasn't that life on board the airship was boring. There was always something that needed to be done. But the things that needed doing quickly became monotonous.

She was used to long spells of boredom. She had done nothing but walk all day for so long before reaching the capital city, and always through grasslands that did indeed change, but only very, very slowly.

And she was used to having long spells of boredom jarringly punctuated with moments of something close to terror. On her travels through the grasslands, those had been almost entirely due to bandits, but a variety of wild animals had made their own contributions. Nothing so terrifying as the jungle cats that flew through the trees, screaming and leaving acrid pools of their own piss as a warning, but potentially lethal all the same.

In the airship, this was always a weather thing. So far, they'd never been caught in a storm, although they'd seen signs of a few on the horizon south of their position. But the wind was always something to be reckoned with. And it liked to change suddenly, without warning, pitching the airship about faster than either Tristan or Lafayette could react to. Dieter was always there. Before he was even called for, he'd be there to take the wheel, but each time he told them they'd gotten lucky. Even when the airship had spun three-quarters of the way around, he insisted that had been a mild gust.

Turning around was no big problem, he said. It was when the wind tried to force them either too high up or too low down that they were in trouble. And that hadn't happened.

Yet.

The main reason airships never flew north to the Arctic region wasn't that it was dangerous. It was because no people lived there, and there was nothing of value to acquire there. Still, the weather was definitely on the list of reasons to stay south of the ice floes.

But, flying aside, there were so many other things about life on the airship that were jarring and new to Lafayette.

For one, her days were very regimented, which was something she wasn't used to. Her parents had left her to her own devices for most of her life, letting her explore and learn things as her whims dictated. Most of what they taught her was forbidden, from books they had to keep hidden, and so she had been compelled to be careful about when she accessed them. But other than that, she woke, ate, worked, and slept on whatever schedule she felt like keeping.

But that didn't work on the airship. They had a strict rotation at the helm, which meant a rotation for who was sleeping. And the eight hours a day when she wasn't doing either of those two things she spent writing everything she could remember from her parents' books in her new journals.

She wrote until her hand cramped, and then pressed on to write some more. And there was always a ticking clock inside her head. How many days until they reached their destination. How many days they could search once they got there. How many days until they reached civilization again.

All of those days together was still not enough for her to get down on paper everything she knew before she started to forget things. It was a constant pressure.

And when her hand simply couldn't hold the pen any longer, she turned her attention back to the stolen tablet, reading entry after entry of the young engineer's diary. Even though very little was of any use to her.

The young engineer in question had provided them with the map of the crashed ships that had been the missing key, the thing that had helped Lafayette and Tristan piece together all the other maps that her father had collected over his lifetime. They knew where the other crashed ships were now, more or less precisely. Lafayette would honor their engineer ancestor's memory forever for that.

And from things she said, Lafayette gathered that she had been quite a talented engineer, on a career fast track, well regarded by her peers and superiors both.

But the problem was, so very little of what she wrote was about engineering, or the history of her people, or anything Lafayette found usable or even interesting.

No, what this young engineer had been most interested in was gossip. And frequently gossip of the most salacious variety.

Lafayette had kept journals throughout her life. She had used them to make sense of everything she learned, to track what she knew and what she wanted to know more about. Her parents' journals had been much the same.

It never even occurred to her to use precious resources like paper, ink, or even just time to record highly detailed speculations about the private lives of all the people around her. Why would she even care?

But this young engineer had cared a lot. She suffered (and she used that word, "suffered," every time) so many crushes, none of them requited. But each crush, before it flamed out in the end, was subject to all sorts of imaginings of what might happen between the two of them if this one, finally, was the one that worked out.

Lafayette wondered, sometimes, how this woman's life had worked out in the end. She had been on board the ship that had become the heart of the capital city when it had come down in the middle of the grasslands. Lafayette felt certain she had survived that experience. She had probably lived a long, full life among the first settlers on this new world. She likely got married at some point. Maybe she had even had children.

For all Lafayette knew, she was reading the diary of one of her own direct ancestors. She didn't know. This diary had been left behind on the ship, but perhaps living on the surface this woman had written other, more mature diaries. Diaries now thoroughly lost to time.

But given the nature of most of the writing, Lafayette rather hoped they weren't actually related. Reading this woman's yearning fantasies about what seemed to be every person she met at some point felt enough like a violation without touching the idea that they might actually be related, however distantly.

Late on the fourth day of their journey northward, Lafayette was sitting on the stool in the corridor, reading from the tablet, her hand throbbing from another long day of putting pen to paper. Tristan was yawning at the controls, and Kora was napping at his feet. Dieter, in the back, was buried so deeply inside his bedroll under the table that only the very top of his dark hair was visible in the dying light of the setting sun.

The entry Lafayette was reading had started promisingly enough. The engineer had been assigned to a work group that was investigating an engine problem, and she had even delved more than once into the topic. The words she used were hard for Lafayette to parse, and she was sure she wasn't grasping the concepts this woman was short-handing at all. But that didn't mean she couldn't with a bit more studious thought.

She was just about to bookmark the entry for later reference when the text took a decidedly graphic turn. The engineer had a new crush, one she knew could go nowhere because the man in question was both her boss and was already married. But that only seemed to encourage her to fantasize more about what she would never have.

"Interesting reading?" Tristan suddenly asked, making Lafayette jump and scramble to turn off the reader. Although she had yet to teach him how to read the language, so it wasn't like he knew what had been displayed there on its screen for all to read.

"It was almost helpful," Lafayette said. "Then it wasn't."

He gave her a look like he knew she was evading the question. And she could feel the flaming heat of her own cheeks. She didn't dare duck into the toilet closet to check in the mirror there, but she wouldn't be surprised if her cheeks were as brightly red as the tips of her hair.

Then he turned his attention back to the controls, making a visual sweep of all the gauges and the horizon outside before turning back to Lafayette.

"I didn't realize how much time flying was going to take," he said with a chagrined smile. "I thought we'd have more time to study together."

"If we find the ship, we'll have all the time we need," she said. "We can be on the same schedule and everything."

"Won't that be nice," he said, crossing his arms as he leaned back against the doorway to smile down at her.

This gondola that was their entire world now was so tiny. He was half inside the cockpit still, and yet there wasn't enough room for him to stand there. Not without the entire side of his leg pressed up against hers as she sat on the stool, tablet still perched on her lap.

"Perhaps I can help with reading lessons," Kora said, although her doggy eyes only opened to the tiniest slits. "When you are sleeping and Dieter is flying, Tristan and I have a little time together we could spend with that tablet."

"Oh, I don't think this is a good place to start," Lafayette said, and wished there was a way she could will her blood not to rush back to her cheeks again.

"Too technical?" Tristan guessed. She couldn't quite tell if he was teasing her or not. But he couldn't be, could he? She hadn't told any of them what she'd been reading in that diary.

"Something like that," she said as evenly as she could.

"We'll find other tablets on the ship, I'm sure," Tristan said.

"Yes. Of course," Lafayette readily agreed.

"There will be classrooms there," Kora said. "They will have just the thing for us to start with. And we're only another day away."

"Exactly," Lafayette said.

"You people need to stop talking like this is a sure thing," Dieter grumbled from under the table.

"Sorry. We didn't mean to wake you," Lafayette said. Tristan ducked back inside the cockpit as if afraid of getting caught by Dieter standing halfway in the corridor.

"You didn't wake me," Dieter said with a sigh as he crawled out of his bedroll. "I'm just saying. We could spend the next eight days searching and be forced to go home empty-handed."

"I don't want to start with that attitude," Lafayette said grumpily.

But he pinned her down with a stare that quelled her. And that was before he'd even gotten to his feet where he could properly tower over her perched on the stool.

"Be optimistic," he told her as if daring her to do so. "But don't act like failure isn't an option. It is, frankly, the most likely outcome."

"We all know that, Diet," Tristan said. "But we've come so far, fleeing Central Planning on foot and in the air. Can't we have a little bit of hope that it will all be worthwhile?"

"Hope all you want," Dieter said. "Just promise me, when our eight days are up and we have to turn around and head home again, I'm not going to have to argue with you two that it has to be done."

"We're not going to argue," Tristan said at once. "It's your ship. It's your call."

Dieter nodded, but his eyes never left Lafayette.

"When eight days are up, the ship goes back," was all Lafayette could bring herself to promise.

Dieter narrowed his eyes at her, like he knew exactly what she had and hadn't said. But in the end he just nodded his acceptance then turned to the kitchenette part of the gondola to fix himself a little food and a lot of coffee.

Not that she considered it much of a hope to hold on to, but if, when the eight days were up, she didn't feel like it was impossible to find the ship, she'd totally have Dieter drop her off on the ice with her share of the remaining food and all the cold-weather gear that still remained stowed, untouched, in the crates under the windows.

Some of their ancestors had walked away from here, after all. If she had to, she could do it too.

But she kind of hoped that, at the very least, Tristan would stay with her.

CHAPTER 8

Lafayette sat on her usual perch at the back of the gondola on top of the supply crates. It was cold sitting that close to the window, even though that glass was thicker than any she had ever seen in her life. She had dug into some of their cold-weather gear and was now wearing a set of thermal underwear under her cargo pants, shirt and vest. The thick waffle-patterned cotton covered her from ankles to wrists and far enough up her neck to touch her ears, and she had on an even thicker pair of socks as well as a pair of hiking boots so heavy they made the pair her father had given her seem almost flimsy by comparison.

Still, it was cold that close to the window. Or maybe it was the sight of all that bluish-gray ice dusted over with drifts of whiter gray snow.

Or maybe it was just her mood.

Dieter had piloted them to the exact spot they'd marked on their map, but there was nothing there. Just the same fields of ice they'd been looking down at since leaving the ocean behind half a day before.

But they had mentally prepared for that. And Dieter, without a single sarcastic comment, had just set about flying in an ever-widening spiral, circling the position where they expected to find the ship and increasing the diameter of their search area with each rotation.

But after seven days, even Lafayette was starting to think this was a hopeless endeavor. And she really hated the cold. She was wearing more layers of clothing than she ever had in her life, but it was like her nose never warmed up. She was constantly sniffling, and she knew the tip of her nose stayed bright red.

And so did her cheeks. She could probably safely peruse the engineer's tablet again without worry that her face would give her reaction to the text away. But that would mean looking away from the ice fields, which she could only bear to do when her eyes were watering too much from the unrelenting intensity of the sunlight reflecting off all that whiteness.

Given the rigor of the flying involved, constantly changing position in and out of the wind, Dieter was the only one in the cockpit these last seven days. Which meant that every night they had to stop so he could rest. But, given that very little could be seen at night, making continuing the search pointless anyway, Lafayette hadn't objected.

The airship had harpoon guns built into the corners of the gondola. They fired wickedly barbed steel harpoons down into the ice below, trailing long cables behind. Once the harpoons were embedded, Dieter fired up the winches that pulled the airship more or less steadily down to a position just off the ground. It was as safe as they could get with no one on the ground to help them make a lot more ropes attached to the balloon itself fast to the ground.

The weather was the one thing they still had going for them. The winds were gentler than Dieter had expected, although if anything that just made him more nervous. Like the weather was tricking them all, luring them into a trap.

Still, if they were going to spend all day flying in circles, and all night only kind of tethered to the ground, calm winds were almost more than they could've hoped for.

Not that it was making any difference. They were wrapping up the seventh day now. One more day of searching even farther from the original position marked on the map, and then they would have to give up. They would have to go home.

Home. That wasn't a word that really had any meaning for Lafayette anymore. Not with her mother dead, her father trapped in orbit, and her onetime guardian Uche Okafo in prison somewhere. Where was she even going to go?

Lafayette had been sitting with her chin propped on her drawn-up knees as she watched the ice passing below them, but the raw despair in her thoughts had her burying her face into her knees. Sitting like that, her own hot breath warmed her nose, if only a little.

And yet, she wasn't doing her job searching if she wasn't looking out the window. She took a few ragged breaths, then lifted her face to put her chin back on her knees.

Nothing but ice. She didn't even think there was any land under there. Just ice over ocean, and who knew how deep the ocean was?

"Time to switch?" Tristan asked her from where he sat at the games table, scribbling away at his journal. He didn't stop writing. She could still hear the nib of his pen scratching on the page. But she thought she felt his gaze on her, if only briefly between words.

"No, I'm good," she said. Although her eyes were starting to water a little. Well, she would have days and days to rest them after tomorrow, wouldn't she?

She listened to the scratching of his pen as she watched the patterns of gray, blue and white go by, until she heard him drop the pen with a hiss of frustration. He would be rubbing the cramp from his hand now, she knew. She did the same whenever he was at the window.

For a moment, the only sound was the soft murmur of Kora's voice up in the cockpit. Lafayette had no idea what she chattered about all day, but she never ceased speaking to Dieter as he piloted the airship. She only rarely heard Dieter's voice making a monosyllabic response before Kora's voice would carry on in a storytelling singsong. But Lafayette supposed that the incessant chatter kept Dieter from dozing off at the controls.

Then Tristan heaved a sigh, shut his journal with something just short of a slam, then climbed up onto the crates by Lafayette's side.

As always, there wasn't quite enough room for two people to fit. But Lafayette shifted closer to the window beside her and pulled her knees up a little tighter to make room for him. Her left side was now just that much colder, being closer to that window. But the warmth of his body pressed against her right side more than made up for it.

"Still nothing," Tristan said, not quite lifting his intonation into a question.

"I don't know how ice works," Lafayette admitted. "The ships hitting the ground left craters, but if you broke through ice that long ago, wouldn't the ice just reform over it? Would we even be able to see it now?"

"I don't know either," Tristan said. "But I'm afraid you might be right about that. We'd have to get under that ice somehow. If it really is just water under there. But I don't know how we'd do it."

"There are boats that can submerge," Lafayette said. "My father showed me pictures of them."

"Pictures in books are one thing," Tristan said. "An actual machine that can do it? That still exists from before? That's something else."

"I would've said the same about this not so long ago," Lafayette said, raising her hands to indicate the airship around them. "But even if it's real, I don't know where we'd find one. Unless Dieter's family has some of those too."

"At this point, nothing about Dieter's family could surprise me," Tristan said. "I mean, even the fact that he has a family, let alone such a huge family, is still a surprise to me."

They fell silent for a moment, the only sound the rise and fall of Kora's voice. Well, that and the ever-present drone of the engines that were always subtly vibrating the walls of the gondola. But it was almost like she had ceased to hear that sound anymore. It was too much a part of the background of her world now.

It was going to be positively deafening, all the things she would hear again when those engines shut off.

Her mind focused on that constant drone now, tuning out everything else. She just existed in that noise for the moment, the never-ending regularity of its whining grind.

But her eyes never left the ice field. Although her mind, lost in the noise, started picking out patterns in the ice to match. Was it really all the same thing? No, obviously it wasn't. At night, when the harpoon winches pulled them down close to the surface, she had seen how uneven the top of the ice floe really was. What looked smooth from high up became jagged, like the ice was constantly grinding against itself, pushing up bits and shoving other bits deeper down. It would be exhausting, trying to walk over all that.

On the other hand, maybe it was a bit like a fractal. The closer in you looked, it was just the same pattern repeating as you saw from farther away. Her father, in one of his many notebooks, had drawn such a thing, and then boxed part of it off and expanded the box out on the next page, all the way through the entire notebook. It had been hypnotic.

Hypnotic. Lafayette gave herself a shake, forcing herself to stop focusing on the engine drone and the patterns in the ice.

Wait. Patterns in the ice?

"What is it?" Tristan asked. She supposed it was the sudden tensing of her body, which he could feel as they sat pressed together. But it was kind of like he was reading her mind.

Lafayette just gave him a long look. She was giddy, bursting with sudden enthusiasm. But the rational part of her mind knew it was way too soon to feel this optimistic about what she was thinking. It was a hypothesis only. Not even a theory. She had yet to test it.

"Dieter!" she cried out instead of explaining herself to Tristan. Tristan yelped in alarm as she scrambled over him to get off the crates and make her lurching way to the cockpit. Not that Dieter's flying was ever anything less than smooth. But she'd been sitting in the same position for too long. Her legs had gone to sleep from her hips down. An odd sensation, but not one she wanted to linger on in that moment.

"Lafayette! Did you see something?" Kora asked as Lafayette gripped the door frame and leaned into the cockpit. Dieter was looking at her half in amusement but half in concern. Well, she supposed she looked odd, not quite able to stand on her own two feet just yet.

Then the pins and needles started, and she sucked in an involuntary breath.

"Are you hurt?" Dieter asked, dropping the amused half of his look at once.

"No, I'm just—" But this was no time for a long explanation about her numb limbs. "I need you to go higher. I need to see this ice field from a higher position. Like, way higher."

"Way higher?" Dieter repeated with an arched brow. Like he was mocking her lack of precision.

"As high as we can go," she said.

"Let me explain to you why that's not a great idea," Dieter said. "Let's start with the problem of replacing the ballast out here in the middle of nowhere—"

"As high as you can safely go," Lafayette interrupted his lecture to clarify. Then, as pleadingly as she could, she said, "Please, Dieter. I need to see something."

Dieter regarded her for a moment, then turned and gave the same attention to the controls before him.

"As high as I safely can," he finally said, to her immense relief. "But only for as long as I safely can. The winds are different up there, and the sun above the clouds is going to heat up the gas in the balloon—"

"I trust you," Lafayette said, interrupting him again. "Just, please."

"What do you think we'll see?" Tristan asked as he joined her crowding the doorway to the cockpit.

"I think… I hope…" But she was too afraid to say anything out loud. Because what if she was wrong? Not that she thought Dieter or Tristan would judge her for making a guess that didn't play out.

No, she was just superstitious enough to be afraid that saying a thing out loud would make it less likely to come to pass. Which was crazy. That wasn't how the world worked.

Still, she held her tongue.

And her breath, as the airship around her started to rise up higher into the air. Now the details of the ice fields below were even harder to make out.

And yet, like with a fractal, a new pattern started to emerge. This was very far removed from the close-up look of the ground, with its jagged breaks and fissures.

But it was also removed from the smooth-appearing surface she had been staring at for the last seven days.

Tristan gasped, and she realized he had seen what she had hoped to, but before her watering eyes could focus on it.

Then she heard Dieter mumble something under his breath. The word was profane, but the tone was all wonder.

Lafayette closed her eyes for several heartbeats, waiting for the sun-dazzled starbursts to fade from her vision to leave her in the darkness behind her eyelids.

Then she opened them again to lean forward towards the window. Dieter, without complaint, jammed himself against the controls to the left of the cockpit so she could just squeeze past him.

Now she saw it for herself. The blue she had been seeing mixed with the white and gray was so much clearer here at this altitude. She was sure it was still technically broken, like when someone wrote with a pen that was rapidly running out of ink.

But like when someone wrote with such a pen and the letters were still recognizable up to a point only just before the ink went dry, the broken bits of blue still described a clear image.

It was a circle. A jagged circle they had been crossing again and again during their search. It hadn't been apparent from close up, but from up here she could see it.

"The edges of the crater," Lafayette said, almost giddy with joy. "It has to be. It's all covered over with ice again now, but somewhere inside that blue circle is what we're looking for."

Tristan whooped with delight, throwing his arms around Lafayette in a sloppy kind of hug. Then they were hopping together, as much as the cramped space would allow.

But Dieter just said, "Fantastic," in his most deeply sarcastic tone. "And I suppose you have a plan to find something trapped under who knows how many tons of ice?"

CHAPTER 9

t was still a few hours before sunset, but Dieter didn't just bring them back down to their usual search elevation. He brought them all the way down within the range of the harpoon lines and anchored the ship down for the night.

Then all three of them did something they had yet to do since coming aboard the ship days before. They sat down together around the games table. Tristan had warmed up a thick beef stew as well as cups of the gritty coffee, well sweetened. But Lafayette sipped at the beverage to get its warmth inside of her. And she barely picked at the stew. It was good, but she was far from hungry.

Dieter, on the other hand, plowed through his entire bowl in large bites taken at a methodical pace. Then he downed his coffee in four long swallows. He wiped his mouth with the back of his hand, pushed back his empty bowl and spoon, and sat back in his chair with his arms crossed.

It was time for the fight to begin.

"We have one day," he said. "One day to search. That's it. Then we have to head back south. We *have* to."

"Of course," Tristan said with a nervous glance towards Lafayette.

"We agreed. Didn't we?" That last was almost a desperate plea. But it was one that Lafayette couldn't let herself hear.

"I had a thought," she said instead.

Tristan groaned and buried his face in his hands. But Dieter just looked ever so slightly amused. Which was to say, the corner of one side of his mouth quirked, if only a little. But he gave her a nod, silently asking her to go on.

"Here's the thing," she said. "I understand about the fuel. And that's not a constraint we can work around. I get that."

"Thank you," Dieter said. She ignored the sarcasm.

"But we don't need to burn the fuel until we're ready to head home, right?" she said. "We can just sit here, right where we are."

Which, she had noticed but didn't add, was at the very center of the blue circle they had seen from the sky. The spot most likely to rest just over the hidden remains of a crashed starship.

She didn't think it was a coincidence. Certainly, Dieter didn't look surprised to hear her words now.

But he said nothing. He just waited for her to continue.

"We have more than enough food," she said.

"You've counted?" Tristan asked. He sounded overwhelmed.

"We have enough food for ten days past the time we'd run out of fuel," she told him. "The water might be more of a problem—"

"But we have cooking fuel to melt snow, and a filtration system to make sure it's drinkable," Dieter said.

Tristan turned to him with surprise. "You planned this too?"

"No," he said with a dry twist to his mouth. "I've just had a lot of time to guess what Lafayette was planning."

"So you know I'm right," Lafayette said with relief.

But that relief was coming a little too soon, to judge from the stony look on Dieter's face. "You're right about the food and water," he conceded. "And, yes, if we don't head back until we have the same six days of food left to match our remaining fuel for the airship engines, then yes, that leaves us ten more days to sit on the ground and search on foot."

"All right," Lafayette said. But her relief didn't come back. There was still something he was going to say, in his own sweet time.

But it was Tristan who spoke next. "Without the engines running, will the balloon deflate or something?"

"No," Dieter said. "In fact, time on the ground will give me time to check on the integrity of the balloon's interior and exterior. Which would be a good idea before journeying home. There could be damage, just small problems. But small problems can become big problems with frightening rapidity. I'd appreciate a few days to look everything over before we head out over open water again."

"Okay," Lafayette said. "So, what, then?"

"I mentioned cooking fuel," Dieter said.

"I caught that," Tristan said. "So that means no electrical power without the engines running?"

"We can work around that, if we have enough cooking fuel," Lafayette said.

"More than enough for cooking and heating water," Dieter said. "Not enough for heating the interior of the gondola. It's going to get cold. And these walls are thick, but they're mostly metal. They aren't going to insulate us from the cold up here."

Lafayette chewed at her lip. She hated the cold. Just feeling it radiate through the windows, through all the layers of her clothing and down into her bones, had made the last few days a nuisance of never quite being comfortable.

But it was a price she was willing to pay to get ten more days to find that ship. And get to her father.

"It's colder than you think," Dieter said, as if her thoughts were written on her face. "But we have heavier gear. We're going to have to put all of it on, mittens and face coverings and everything. And we're going to have to keep them on. We're going to have to sleep in parkas, because, as nice as these bedrolls are, they aren't warm enough for this environment."

"I can do it," Lafayette said. "Ten days of discomfort is something I can live with."

"How cold can it be, really?" Tristan asked. He was shooting for lighthearted, but Dieter just gave him a pitying look. Tristan blanched, but said nothing.

"I tell you what," Dieter said, getting up from the table to start moving crates around. "We have to secure this ship better if we're going to be parked for ten days. And I'll need your help with the mooring lines. So let's get suited up and head outside. Then you'll know for yourself just how cold it can be."

Lafayette looked down at her thick cargo pants with the thermal underwear underneath. And she was wearing incredibly thick socks, her favorite new item of clothing if she was being honest, although she'd never discount the benefits of such a solid pair of boots. Surely all she needed was a parka and mittens? And whatever Dieter meant by face covering.

But the first thing Dieter thrust at her was yet another pair of pants. Coveralls, actually, with a bib in front and thick straps to hold them on over her shoulders.

"Trust me," he said, thrusting a similar pair at Tristan before shaking out his own pair. "The wind can cut right through what we're wearing now."

"You've never been this far north before," Tristan said. Not quite a question.

"No, but I've been further north than you," Dieter said as he stepped into his pants and slipped his arms through the straps. "And I've been on top of a few mountains."

"I've seen mountains with snow on top of them," Lafayette found herself saying. Which sounded stupid, she knew. She'd been nowhere near those mountains. She'd seen them like a smudge on the horizon.

But Dieter just gave her a nod. "Snow and ice as well, although that's hard to discern from a distance."

Lafayette got into the coveralls, but the straps kept slipping down off her arms. Well, it wasn't the first time she'd wished she could be just a little bit taller. But Tristan came around the corner of the table to help her adjust the length of the straps as Dieter dove back into the crate and came up with long, thick scarves. Not the wispy, diaphanous things that Lafayette was used to calling scarves. These were made of scratchy wool, and as Dieter demonstrated, were worn wrapped several times around the neck.

"You don't want air on your skin if you can help it," he explained even as he handed her a pair of tinted goggles. They fit low over her nose and high over her forehead, and would surely keep the air off of most of her face.

But the tint would've really come in handy over the last few days spent staring out at blinding snow. If only she'd examined all the crates rather than just counting up their foodstuffs.

"Get the scarf up higher, over the bottom of your face," Dieter said, his voice muffled through his own scarf. He reached across the table to adjust hers before thrusting a fur-lined hat with earflaps over her head.

"Shouldn't this go on first?" Lafayette asked as she fumbled to fasten the hat's strap under her chin around the layer of scarf Dieter had just dragged up there.

But all he said was, "Trust me."

Finally, he handed out the parkas: blue for Tristan, yellow for her, and a red one for himself. Lafayette's was, like the pants, a little too big for her. But that was probably fine. The sleeves covered her hands almost entirely, especially when her arms were down at her sides. She scarcely needed gloves or mittens at all, she thought. But didn't say. When Dieter thrust a pair of mittens at her, she took them without a word and struggled to push her sleeves up and keep them there long enough to get the mittens on. Like the hat, they had straps to keep them secured around her wrists.

Dieter pulled the hood of his parka up over his hat, then cinched its cord tight around his face so that his goggles were all that were visible within the tunnel of red cloth. Tristan and Lafayette did the same.

"I do believe that I shall stay inside," Kora announced from the cockpit.

"I can make something warm for you later, if you change your mind," Dieter told her. "I have some spare materials, and I'm pretty handy with a needle."

"Thank you. For now, I'll keep an eye on things from here."

Dieter fumbled with his mittened hands inside another crate before emerging with a thick fur-lined blanket. He tucked it snugly around Kora in her nest under the controls. Only when he was sure she was comfortable did he open the latches one by one, then put a shoulder against the door to shove it open.

The cold rushed in the moment the door was open, and Lafayette found herself instantly gasping for breath. That cold had penetrated through the parka that was zipped up to the bottom of her nose, past all the layers of woolen scarf, down into the deepest depths of her lungs, and had frozen into ice crystals there.

It *hurt*.

It was freezing every bit of moisture in her nose, her mouth, her throat, her very lungs.

And that was all from its very first touch. She hadn't even inhaled any of it yet.

But Dieter was already outside, trudging across the ice, and Tristan was grasping the doorway to follow.

It was hard moving around. The layers of clothing made her feel big and awkward. Unlike the rest of her clothing, her boots were a perfect fit, but walking on ice was harder than it looked. Mostly because, unlike the few times the water back home had frozen over hard enough to be walked on, this ice was the farthest thing from smooth.

It was slippery, but in raised ridges and toe-tripping crevices all over. Some of it crunched underfoot, but other parts of it didn't. It was hard to tell from step to step how it was going to react to having her weight on it. She just had to take the step and find out.

Then take another step, and find out again.

It was slow going. It took the better part of an hour trudging behind Dieter. Who, to be fair, didn't seem any better at moving over the terrain than Tristan or Lafayette. But he did know what needed to be done to drive the mooring posts like thicker versions of the harpoons deep into the ice, then retrieve the lines his sisters had last touched and secure them to the posts.

They had to do that all around the ship. Because while the harpoons that had held them nightly before had been attached to the gondola, this time it was the balloon itself they were securing.

Lafayette got to appreciate all over again just how enormous the airship was. The awe was almost enough to drown out the misery of the cold, plodding progress they were making.

Almost.

The sun was long gone from the sky by the time they headed back to the gondola. Lafayette quickly found that being fatigued made walking over that ice far more difficult than before, and the darkness certainly didn't help. She stumbled again and again, but somehow she managed to never quite fall on her face. So that was something.

Then they were back inside, and the door was once more latched behind them. They shuffled around the games table one more time, and Lafayette pushed back her goggles and pulled the parka and scarf down from around her mouth to get a proper breath of air.

It didn't hurt quite as bad as that first breath of cold, but it was definitely far colder inside the gondola than it had been when they'd landed. And it was probably going to get colder still.

She felt Dieter's eyes on her, like he was waiting for her to admit how miserable she was. Like he was waiting for her to ask to give up and just head home.

But she would never do that.

She kept the parka unzipped to the base of her throat, undid the strap of the hat, and tucked the layers of scarf over her face under her chin. Then she gave Dieter what she truly hoped was her brightest smile.

"Tomorrow, we start searching," she said. "I can hardly wait."

Dieter just gave her words a nod, but she knew that gesture for what it was.

Respect. Grudging respect, but respect all the same.

She would take it.

CHAPTER 10

ife inside an airship sitting on the ice was far more arduous than life inside an airship up in the sky. And each day seemed to find a way for everything to get just a little bit worse.

First, they couldn't cook inside the gondola. The space was too cramped, and with no engines there was no ventilation. It wasn't safe to burn fuel and cook over an open flame inside. So, Dieter had used empty crates and a heavy-duty tarp to build a structure of sorts to act as an outdoor kitchen.

So now, even if you just wanted a hot mug of coffee, you had to gear up for the weather and go outside to heat up the water in the makeshift tent.

Tristan had found a couple of thick canteens that could keep hot beverages hot for a surprising length of time. So he took to making a large batch of coffee in the morning to fill the canteens, and they rationed it out the rest of the day.

And they had several jars of nut butter. It was like the perfect food, rich and filling but required no preparation of any kind.

So, of course, they depleted all their stores of it by the third day. And then they were back to heating water to rehydrate their shelf-stable rations.

Lafayette couldn't remember a time when she'd been so ravenously hungry all the time. Not even when she'd been trekking from the crater where she'd lost her father to the capital city had she been so desperately hungry. Granted, moving over the treacherously uneven ground wearing extremely heavy clothing was exhausting. But also, she was pretty sure the cold itself was sapping her energy.

It certainly felt that way.

Any sign of the ship remained as elusive as ever. But at least she was succeeding in her secondary goal. She wasn't letting any of her discomfort and annoyance emerge from her. She wasn't complaining about anything, not even once.

Which, given the track the thoughts inside her head kept taking, was really saying something. She had never felt so miserable in her life. And, with no sign of the ship and day after day eating away at their food stores faster than she'd anticipated because she wasn't the only one struggling with constant hunger, all of that misery felt like it wasn't even leading to anything good or useful.

She felt herself edging closer to despair.

But she fought it back. She tuned out the negative thoughts in her head and forced herself to keep moving. To eat enough to fuel her body, then use that fuel to trudge over ridge after ridge of ice, searching for any sign at all that somewhere beneath the soles of her boots her goal still lay hidden.

Out of reach. She was so close; she knew she was. But she was starting to fear it would remain out of reach. How was she going to tunnel through ice, anyway? She had no plan beyond using the food stores to keep searching.

Dieter mostly stayed with the airship. Not that he wasn't trying to help with the search, but he didn't want to leave his family's ship unattended. The winds remained calm, but the longer that condition lasted, the more nervous he became about the inevitable storm he was sure was going to follow. So he stayed always within eyesight of his balloon, ready to respond to any change in their situation.

Which Lafayette could only hope wouldn't mean taking to the air even if she and Tristan were still out on the ice, searching for signs of the crashed ship. But she couldn't bring herself to straight out ask him what he intended to do.

Tristan, at least, was always by her side. They walked together, scanning the barren landscape through their tinted goggles, but seldom speaking. It was like speaking was too much of an effort. Especially as being heard through so many layers of clothing both over their mouths and over their ears was just one more exhausting thing on a long list of exhausting things.

But it was nice, working together. The conditions were terrible, and unlike in the cramped interior of the gondola, there wasn't even any casual touching, little moments of warmth she hadn't even realized she had looked forward to every day.

Maybe that engineer with her fantasy-filled diary was having a bad influence on her; Lafayette didn't know. She just found herself longing for a moment alone in some normal kind of space, just her and Tristan and something a lot more like a normal amount of clothing between them.

"I looked at our stores this morning," Tristan suddenly said out of nowhere. As usual when one of them spoke, Lafayette stopped walking and turned to face him. Not that she could see his mouth to understand him better or anything. But it was easier to hear if she was putting her full attention on it.

And she could use a break from the walking.

"I did too," she admitted. "I know what you're going to say. It's never going to last ten days. Or, I guess it's been five. We don't have five more. I'd guess more like three."

"That's assuming we slow up eating when we start the trip back," Tristan said.

"Sure we will," she said, flapping her arms at her side in a vague gesture that encompassed the world around them. "We won't be walking through this anymore. If we're feeling weak still, we can just take extra time for sleep."

Which sounded so good right now. But, without quite saying it out loud, she and Tristan both had been getting up before dawn to fill up on breakfast before spending all the hours of sunlight trudging around. Only after dark did they fill up on dinner before shivering themselves to sleep to start the whole process over again the next day.

She'd love not to walk. Even writing all day in her journal would be less tiring than this was.

"Still, we're not going to make five more days," Tristan said. "And besides the amount of food left, I know that Dieter is getting really worried about the change in weather he thinks is coming."

"I've sensed that too," Lafayette said. "He's not going to wait until the storm's here to tell us we're heading out, is he?"

"I don't think it would be a good idea if he did," Tristan said. "We have to be gone *before* the storm comes, don't you think? Rather than try to fly away from here through one?"

"I know you're right," Lafayette said.

"I'm sorry," Tristan said, taking a step closer to her. She could see his eyes now, through the dark tint of his goggles. And she supposed he could see hers as well.

"Well," she said, her throat trying to choke off her words. But she pressed on. "It's not like we're finding anything."

"If we did, I'm afraid it would still be inaccessible," Tristan said. "The ship must've hit the ice, created that crater we saw from above, then that crater filled with ice again. Maybe the heat from the impact melted the water, and then it froze again?"

"Or it was a slower process, because it's one that's been ongoing for centuries," Lafayette sighed. "It's not like I haven't been thinking all this too."

"I know," Tristan said. "It's your father, though. We have to try until it just isn't possible to try anymore. I get it."

Lafayette just nodded mutely.

"Family is important," Tristan said. Lafayette tipped her head to one side, communicating a silent question about where he was going with this statement. "It's important to Dieter, too. You know his family knows how much fuel they gave us. And how far we were going. And when we were due back."

"They might be starting to expect us back by now, but it's just the front end of a window of time," Lafayette said. "They won't get really worried for a while longer yet."

"No, you're right," Tristan said. "It's just, Dieter doesn't have a way of reaching them. To let them know that we're still all right. Not without drawing all of Central Planning right down on top of us."

"That was true even before we left," Lafayette said. "His family knows that too."

"I know," Tristan said.

"You want to get back too, don't you," Lafayette said. "That's what this is all about. You're worried about Dieter."

"I'm worried about you too," Tristan said, and took another half step forward. Then he tipped his head down to hers, so that their foreheads were touching. Or, at least, their goggles were. His mittened hands clutched at the sleeves of her parka.

Lafayette had never felt such a close gesture that, really, didn't seem to involve her at all. It was very odd. And yet, at the same time, charming.

"Why are you worried about me? I'm fine," Lafayette said.

"No, you're not," he said, but there was a fond smile in his voice, she knew it. "You're trying hard not to show it, but you're ready to give up too. I know it's killing you, and I don't expect you to admit that I'm right. But I'm right. You can't keep doing this. I just hope we run out of food before your mind snaps from the strain of maintaining optimism."

"I'm not that bad," Lafayette said.

"You're holding it together," he said. "But barely."

"I just need a few more days," Lafayette said.

"Lafayette, we're not finding anything," he said softly, so softly she almost couldn't hear him even as close as he was standing to her. It was as if the cold itself was trying to take his words away before she could hear them. "Do you really think that's about to change?"

"Yes," she said, lifting her chin as if in defiance of the entire world. "Yes, I think it is. I don't know how, but I know it will. It will change. We're going to find something."

"How can you know that?" he asked almost shrilly.

"Because it always has," she said. She hoped the muffling effect of their layers of clothing would hide the fact that she was tearing up. So that the fierce edge of the defiance she was clinging to was all that came through.

But he was still close enough for her to see his eyes, and she saw the sadness in them.

"I wish I could feel the same, Lafayette. I really do," he said.

His mittened hands squeezed the sleeves of her parka one last time. Then he stepped away. And it was like the cold all around her rushed to take his place, to squeeze at her and whisper in her ear. To steal away all the warmth she had left.

Lafayette curled her mittened hands into fists and took a deep breath, trying to release an entire ball of emotions in her chest without taking the time to pick the ball apart and identify everything it contained.

It was a lot. A lot of feelings.

But she didn't have the energy for any of them. And she was running out of time as well.

Slowly, she released the tension from her fists. Then she untensed her shoulders, and shook out her arms.

She took a single step, closer to Tristan. She wasn't going to try to argue her point of view. She was too tired for that. But she hoped that if she just kept walking, he would keep walking too. And if she was the only one still searching for signs of the lost ship, that was all right. If all he did was walk beside her, that was all she needed to keep walking herself.

She took a second step closer to Tristan, who was turned away from her, not looking at her at all.

He took a step himself. Was it a step away from her, or a step continuing their walk? She wasn't sure. All she could see was the back of his hood.

Then he took another step, and with a silent suddenness, he flashed out of sight. One second she was looking at the back of his bright blue parka, and the next there was nothing in front of her but snow and ice.

Snow and ice that carried on forever in jagged, overlapping ridges, all the way to the distant horizon where it met the sky.

The sky that was darkening with a growing storm.

CHAPTER 11

Lafayette dashed to where Tristan had been standing, then skidded to a halt as she realized just how foolish rushing would be in this moment.

There was only one place he could've gone. Only one way he could've disappeared so quickly. And if she wasn't careful, she would follow right after him.

And Dieter and Kora had no idea where the two of them were right now.

Her heart was hammering in her chest, but she forced her breathing to slow down. Then she edged forward, shuffling step by shuffling step.

And saw what she already knew she would see: a fissure in the ice. Larger than the others. Large enough to swallow Tristan up whole.

"Tristan?" she called as she got down on her knees on the rough ice and tried to peer down the chasm. It was narrow. If his shoulders had been angled just a little bit differently, he would've been hung up very near the surface. Near enough for her to reach down and help him get back out.

But even with all the bulky cold-weather gear, his body had been slim enough to slip down that narrowest of channels. And who knew how deep that went?

"Tristan!" she called again, louder this time. Then she had to force herself to sit quietly, to soften her breathing enough to hear any sound he might be making far down there.

She heard something, faintly. She thought it might be her name.

She hoped it wasn't just her imagination.

She needed help. There was nothing she could do to get to Tristan. Not even the unfurled length of her scarf would be enough to reach him if he was so deep she couldn't hear his words.

Lafayette got to her feet, then started digging through the pockets of her parka. She had accumulated things over the last few days of hiking. Food wrappers, tissues, a pocket tool. But none of that was helpful now.

In the end, it *was* her scarf that she turned to. Not as a makeshift rope. It still wasn't long enough for that. But, being a bright shade of yellow, it made an excellent flag. Not that she had a pole to hang it from, but that was okay. She wasn't going to forget this location entirely. And their boots had left marks in the looser bits of snow cover on the ice. Enough for her to find the path again. She only needed a marker to be sure of the location of the fissure.

She found a few protrusions of ice that she could kick free with her heavy boots, then made a small cairn from them, weighing down the scarf with another of the stone-like chunks of ice.

"Tristan! I'll be right back with help!" she yelled into the fissure, although she doubted he could hear her any better than she could hear him.

Then she ran back to the airship. There was never any worry about finding that.

To her surprise, she was only halfway back to it when she saw Dieter and Kora jogging to meet her. Dieter was all geared up the same as Lafayette and Tristan were, although when he was working on things inside the airship he usually left the bulky parka off and wore only the thinnest pair of gloves.

Lafayette had known that Dieter had been working on cold-weather gear for Kora. He had told her about it when she and Tristan had come back into the gondola at night. But by that time of day she was so exhausted she had only nodded along to the words she was half-listening to, then crashed in her bedroll without really thinking anything through.

But he had geared up Kora very nicely for the weather. She had a hat of her own, with goggles sized for a small child over her eyes. Two children's parkas had been cut and sewn together so that she had sleeves for all four of her legs. And even her paws were covered, with boots fashioned from two pairs of gloves.

"We heard you yelling," Dieter said when he was close enough to be heard. Which was so close that even as he continued speaking, he took Lafayette by the elbow and pivoted her around to head her back the way she'd just come.

"Tristan fell into a fissure in the ice," Lafayette told him, pointing with her mittened hand to where her yellow scarf was just visible through the frozen hillocks of ice.

"Is he hurt?" Kora asked, her tone deeply worried.

"I don't know. I think I can hear him calling for me, but I'm not sure," Lafayette said. "The space is so narrow, and it twists off, not just straight down. I can't see very far into it."

"We have plenty of rope on the airship," Dieter said. "And more harpoon launchers with winches if we need them."

"I don't want to shoot a harpoon when I can't even see where Tristan is," Lafayette said.

"Nor do I," Dieter assured her.

They had reached the spot on the ice. Dieter didn't need Lafayette to warn him, though. He slowed down far sooner than she did, approaching in a cautious shuffle before dropping to his own knees to examine the fissure.

"Rotten luck," he grumbled, too loudly to be just to himself considering how hard it was to be heard through all their layers. "He must've been standing just right when he went down or he would've hung up here where we could get to him."

"I was thinking the same thing," Lafayette said.

Kora, even more cautious than the two of them, glided closer to the fissure using her hover disk at a higher setting. Her paws were dangling, propelling her forward with one little swipe of a booted toe at a time.

"What do you think?" Dieter asked Kora after giving her a moment to absorb everything. "Can you get down there?"

"Get down there?" Lafayette repeated, dumbstruck. She had never even thought of it. But Kora was definitely small enough to fit through that fissure. Even in her parka.

"I can, but it would be wiser to send me down with a tether," Kora said.

"I'll get some rope," Dieter said, edging back from the fissure on his hands and knees before getting up to run back to the airship.

"Are you sure you want to do this?" Lafayette asked Kora. "What if you get stuck?"

"I can't get stuck until I've reached Tristan, as I'm much smaller than he is," Kora said confidently. "If I get stuck with him, then you and Dieter will have to come up with another rescue plan."

"Do you remember saving me? When I fell in that hole back at the crater from the first spaceship?" Lafayette asked. "It was before I put Sameera Adel's construct inside you—"

"Of course I remember," Kora interrupted her to say, sounding offended. But then her tone softened, and in a rare moment the voice speaking to her was entirely Sameera Adel, the teacher from another planet who had taught Lafayette how to read the language of the spaceship people. "Kora was different from other dogs even before I joined with her. All she could say was your name, but I think you already know she meant so many different things when she spoke your name. She had thoughts and feelings more advanced than a normal dog's. And her memories were quite profound."

"I didn't know that," Lafayette said. "Well, I suspected she meant a lot of things when all she was saying was my name. But I didn't think too much about what the world was like from her point of view."

"Perhaps I'll tell you more about it sometime," Kora said, then turned her doggy nose back to the fissure. "When we are not so terribly preoccupied."

Lafayette heard the sound of boots on ice and looked up to see Dieter returning with one of the spare lines for the ship. It was the thinnest of those lines, the ones used with the harpoons and winches, but Lafayette knew just how strong that line was.

"Tie it well, Dieter," Kora instructed as Dieter drew one end of the rope around Kora's middle. His fingers, even in the heavy-duty gloves, were deft as they executed a perfect knot that Lafayette was certain would never come loose. Kora tried to crane her head around to see it, but with the goggles on that was quite impossible.

"Lafayette?" she said.

Lafayette fought the completely inappropriate urge to giggle at this. Kora, back to only saying her name but using it to say everything. But the thought of Tristan, trapped in the ice, getting colder by the minute, killed that urge dead.

"It looks good," Lafayette assured her. "It won't come undone. We'll probably need to cut it free with a knife to get it off you."

Dieter shifted his weight a little. Lafayette couldn't see his face to read his expression, but she could guess at his thoughts, anyway. Needing a knife to cut the rope off Kora was an insult to his knot-tying skills. He could undo whatever he had done, and it annoyed him that Lafayette was suggesting otherwise.

But he didn't say anything out loud.

"Very well," Kora said. "I shall find young Tristan. If he can get his hands onto the rope around my waist, can you pull him up?"

"The two of us together? Surely," Lafayette said.

"Well," Dieter said, too quickly on top of her words.

"Kora can float. She doesn't weigh a thing. The two of us can handle Tristan's weight," Lafayette said, trying not to sound as annoyed as she felt.

"It's not that," Dieter said. "If this fissure twists a lot… I mean, the less straight the course of the rope is, the harder it will be to pull."

"I guess you're right about that," Lafayette admitted.

Kora looked from one of them to the other, her dog eyes blinking behind those tinted goggles.

"Tristan and I will assess the situation," she said at last. "If need be, I'll come back up without him to report to you."

"Perfect," Lafayette said. "But it's going to be dark soon."

Plus there was that storm she had seen. She hadn't mentioned it to

Dieter yet, but she knew he had seen it. He had been watching and waiting for it for so long.

"I'm on my way," Kora said. Then she dove in the hole with all the speed of a prairie rodent taking cover at the first sign of a predator.

"We could use a winch, right?" Lafayette asked Dieter, looking him over to see if he'd hidden one somewhere on his person.

"If we wanted to pull both of Tristan's arms out of his sockets, sure," Dieter said dryly.

Lafayette flinched. She didn't mean to, but she had.

"Sorry," Dieter said. "I know you're worried. But we're going to figure this out."

"We have to," Lafayette said. "There's no one else here to help us."

They lapsed into silence then. Lafayette's knees were growing cold from kneeling on the ice, even through all the insulated layers she had on. It was like the ice could leach the warmth right out of her. But she didn't even dare to shift her weight. She was afraid moving at all would mean not hearing any sound that might come up out of that fissure.

Not that there was any sound coming out of the fissure. All she could hear was the sound of her own breathing, like it was echoing around inside the drawn-up hood of her parka. Dieter's breathing beside her was barely discernible. And the whispers of air around her were too faint to even merit the word "breeze."

Then, all at once, Kora's face burst up out of the ice again. She put two booted paws up on the surface but stopped there, not quite climbing up out of the hole.

"Where's Tristan?" Lafayette demanded.

"Below," Kora said.

"Can't he hold the rope so we can pull him up?" Dieter asked.

"Probably," Kora said, offhandedly. As if that issue were not of primary importance.

"So why isn't he up here?" Lafayette asked.

"The bit here by the surface is the narrowest spot," Kora said as if she hadn't even heard Lafayette's question. "You have pickaxes and things back at the airship, don't you, Dieter? You could break past that point in a jiffy, I should think. Then, the rest is just like one long slide. Like children play on. No trouble at all."

"A slide down to what?" Dieter asked.

"Down to the cavern below," Kora said. "I'm sorry. I'm saying this all out of order. Tristan is waiting for you down there. He is a *bit* hurt, but he says not to worry about that. The important thing is you get down there to him."

"I'll get an axe," Dieter said.

But at the same time, Lafayette demanded, "Why?"

"Oh," Kora said. "He said not to tell you. He wants to show you. But I think, all things considered, you should really try to hurry."

CHAPTER 12

Dieter fetched the axe and made short work of the ice blocking the opening of the tunnel down to Tristan. Even so, the sun was already starting to set by the time he had broken away enough ice for the two of them to fit through it.

But sunset on the ice floe was a weird thing. It was like it happened in slow motion. Or like the sun wanted to hunker down on the horizon but wasn't quite ready to call it a night yet. Either way, it meant they had run out of strong, direct light, but still had a couple of hours of weaker, more diffuse light left.

The storm on the southern horizon was still building there, but moving no closer to them. Overhead, the brightest of the stars were just coming into view. Lafayette knew that even in the middle of the night, the light from those stars and the two moons was enough for her to find the airship. It glowed like a bubble of living silver, impossible to miss.

But the shadows cast by the light from the moons and stars were even more confusing than the shadows cast by the sun. All of those fissures and ridges became even more of a jumble of foot-catching hazards.

And it would be completely dark, down in that hole.

"That's got to do it," Dieter said at last, tossing the axe aside. Lafayette leaned closer to the hole, trying to peer down its length. But there was no sign of Kora, let alone Tristan. And she didn't really know how deep this tunnel ran.

"Here," Dieter said, nudging her arm with some hard object. She sat back and took it from him before she realized what it was. A portable lantern, something like the ones her father had used around his campsite when the two of them had still been traveling together. She had sold every last one of those in exchange for food to get to the capital city, but she wasn't surprised that Dieter, with his traveling and trading family, had access to a different version of the same thing.

"I have one for Tristan too," he said, slapping his own chest gently. "They're sturdy, but not unbreakable. Maybe tuck yours inside your parka until you get to the bottom, just to be sure you don't drop it on the way down."

Lafayette nodded wordlessly, then sucked in a preparatory breath before unzipping her parka. She only opened it just enough to wedge the lantern inside, and only kept it open as long as she needed to, but that was still a great blast of frigid air right on her torso.

At least she had her scarf back, wrapped snugly around her neck and upper shoulders. Dieter had brought a pole with him when he'd retrieved the axe from the airship. Not that there was much chance of losing track of where the hole was now. They had churned up the ice and snow all around it with their boots, plus Dieter had pulled as much ice out when he'd broken it apart as he'd let slide down to the bottom.

"I'll go first," Dieter said.

Lafayette just nodded again. She wondered if it would be warmer down in the ice. It would be out of the wind, only up on the surface there wasn't much of a wind either. So maybe she'd be just as cold there as she was now. Her jaw ached, and she knew it was from the low-key clenching she was always doing to keep her teeth from chattering.

Dieter made a few adjustments to his clothing, then sat down on the ice, putting his feet into the hole. He looked up at Lafayette, but in the dying light of the setting sun and with the tinting of his goggles, Lafayette couldn't see his eyes at all.

Then he was gone, the cloth of his pants and parka whispering against the ice, a soft sound that faded away all too soon.

Then Lafayette was alone. And she felt truly alone, as if her friends were long gone and not just a short slide away from her. The landscape around her was so isolating, so alien, so unwelcoming to what she needed just to stay alive. It was chilling in far more than the simple, literal way.

And yet it was also beautiful. The silvers and blues only grew more lovely as the cold light of the sun slipped away. And as much as she knew it was an illusion, the lines of everything around her felt like they just got sharper, more defined.

Was she actually going to miss this place when they left it? She certainly wouldn't miss the cold. And yet, she felt just a little bit sad at the thought of sailing home again. She knew she'd never see this place again. Why would she ever come back here?

Lafayette tore her eyes away from the world around her and focused just on the hole. The walls of the tunnel through the ice were almost ridged, as if the work of an enormous ice-tunneling worm. But they were smooth ridges, not jagged. This wasn't likely to hurt.

She sat down on the edge of the hole, put her booted feet in first, then pushed her butt off the snowy surface before she had a chance to lose her nerve. She folded her arms over her chest, both to keep them from catching on anything she couldn't see in the dark, but also to add just a little more protection to the lantern inside her parka.

It was the strangest feeling, zipping at what felt like amazing speed, down in a wide spiral, through a darkness her eyes couldn't penetrate. It felt like the ice was closing in around her, but she was sure that was only because she couldn't see it. If it got too narrow for her, Dieter and Tristan both would've been stuck first. She was safe.

But she didn't feel safe.

Then she was in a larger cavern, a cavern she could *see*, sliding across the icy floor on her back for several meters even though the floor had leveled out when she'd left the tunnel behind.

The light was from the two lanterns Dieter had brought down with him, as well as a greener-toned light that Lafayette knew was coming out of Kora's robotic chest. She had found a way to turn her indicator lights up far past the intensity that Lafayette would've thought possible. It gave the ice walls around them an almost algae color, like they were trapped in a frozen sea that was filled with living things suspended inside it.

"It's big enough," Dieter was saying even as Lafayette took a minute after coming to a rest to just lie there, blinking up at the ceiling above her. The ice ceiling. "That's not the problem."

"I'm not saying abandon the airship," Tristan said.

"Oh, I know you're not saying that," Dieter said jauntily.

"Tristan," Lafayette said, rolling over to her hands and knees then pushing herself up to standing. "You're okay?"

"Twisted an ankle, I think, but otherwise fine," Tristan said. Judging from the limp in his step as he came over to her, that twist was more than a "think," but Lafayette didn't call him out on it.

Her brain was far more fixated on the fact that he had uncovered his face and pushed his hood back.

Was it really that much warmer down here?

"There's a storm on the way," Dieter said to Tristan as Lafayette used her awkwardly mittened hands to push her hood back, then shoved the tinted goggles up onto her forehead so she could see better in the lantern-lit darkness of the ice cave.

"You've been saying that for days, though," Tristan said.

"Because it's been brewing for days," Dieter shot back.

"I saw it too," Lafayette said, then pulled down her layers of scarf so her words wouldn't come out quite so muffled. "It's south of us. It didn't look like it was coming this way, yet, but it was definitely getting darker. And not just because the sun was going down. It was like… intense."

"Exactly," Dieter said.

"But isn't this a safer place for us to shelter?" Tristan countered.

Dieter scowled darkly but said nothing.

"We can't risk losing the airship," Lafayette guessed. "It's our only way home. And if we're down here, we won't know when the airship is in trouble."

"Exactly," Dieter said, but more softly this time.

"Can we tie it up closer to the hole?" Tristan asked. "We'd have to move the mooring lines and everything, I know. But honestly, I'd rather be down here during a storm than up in the gondola. For a couple of reasons."

"There is more space down here," Lafayette said. "Would it be safe to cook down here, though?"

"I don't know," Dieter said with a helpless shrug. "It seems big enough, but what do I know?"

"There are other fissures in this ice," Kora told them all. "Smaller ones. Perhaps enough for proper ventilation. But when that storm hits, it won't be possible to cook outdoors either. Not even in the kitchen tent."

"Right," Dieter said with the tone of someone accepting the inevitable. "I'll go up and secure everything on the airship, then run a permanent line from the surface down to here using one of the harpoons and winches. Then we'll all have to work together to move the airship over here and make her fast."

"So we're staying," Tristan said with obvious relief. "Honestly, I was expecting more of a fight on account of the food rations and all."

"We only have enough for one more day plus the trip home," Lafayette said.

"Well, I'd hate to break it to you all, but that became academic at about the same time that Tristan fell down this hole," Dieter said. "That storm is a smear on the southern horizon. It's between us and anywhere we'd try to go. We can't outrun it. We'd be fools to try to run through it."

"So we're stuck here?" Lafayette said.

Dieter just nodded.

"For how long?"

Dieter shrugged. "It could be several days. Maybe all the days we have left of our food supply."

"We should've left sooner," Lafayette said.

"I should've forced that call sooner," Dieter said almost gently. "I was watching the storm, but I was allowing for an unacceptable level of risk. Now we're stuck here. That's on me."

"But we didn't fail," Tristan said. "Don't you see? Maybe we should've given up even a few hours sooner, but if we had, we'd never have found it."

"We found it?" Lafayette asked, peering at the ice around them for the millionth time. But still all she saw was the greenish glow from Kora's light.

"You have to look past the reflection," Tristan said, taking Lafayette by the elbow and guiding her to the narrowest end of the chamber, where the teardrop-shaped space tapered off into the tightest of Vs. Lafayette stared where Tristan was pointing, down and slightly to her left.

At first she thought she was imagining it, just a dark blur of a shape, like the light blue of the ice became a darker smear of color.

Only it definitely *was* a shape. She moved her head from side to side, but while the blue of the ice shifted with her motion, that darker shape did not.

"It's a ship, right?" Tristan said. "I think it's the part of the curve of the wheel of a ship."

"Maybe," Lafayette said. But the rapid beat of her heart would've given her away if he could've heard it.

There was no maybe in her mind. She knew what she was looking at. There was no question. And if she really stared, she thought she could make out the rectangular protrusion of an airlock door. Like the one her father had broken into on the first ship. The one she had followed him through, some days later.

"There's a lot of ice between us and that," Dieter said.

"We have axes," Tristan said.

"And time," Lafayette added.

"But not food to fuel our muscles," Dieter said.

"There's food inside that ship," Lafayette said. "Kora and I can access it. We can stuff ourselves silly, and have heat and proper beds to sleep in and everything. We just have to get through this ice."

"And what else are we going to do while we wait for the storm to pass?" Tristan asked.

Dieter scowled at both of them. But he gave up with an elaborate shrug.

"Half rations," he said. "We move the airship, bring everything we need down here, and then we're on half rations. Everyone will have to find their own ice-axing pace on half rations."

Lafayette wanted to throw her arms around him in the tightest of hugs, but she was pretty sure he'd fight that gesture. So she just grinned at him and sort of danced in place.

But Tristan's brain stayed in a more logical mode. Lafayette knew he was as excited about all of this as she was. But he still managed to utter out the coldest of hard questions.

"And when the storm breaks? What do we do then?" he asked.

"We'll have to reassess," Dieter said. "There are too many variables. How much food is left. How much progress we've made tunneling towards the ship. How much damage the airship takes in this storm. All of it."

His eyes cut a look Lafayette's way. Like he wanted to warn her that reassessment was going to be grim, but he also couldn't bear to burst her enthusiasm.

So Lafayette tamped it down on her own, getting her body to stand still and holding the grin at bay as she gave him a nod of understanding.

And then they started bundling back up, to get to the surface and do all the work that needed to be done in such a hurry.

But Lafayette knew what Dieter hadn't been saying to her. It wasn't that he didn't want to hurt her feelings. That wasn't really something Dieter ever worried about.

It was more like, Lafayette's enthusiasm and the way that Tristan's rose to match it in their best moments together, that energy was going to be all that would get them through the days to come. And Dieter needed it just as much as they did.

Not that he'd ever say so out loud. But Lafayette knew.

It was a responsibility she was prepared to take very seriously.

CHAPTER 13

They made quick work of moving the airship, towing it using the lines until the gondola's door rested just beside the hole in the ice. They used the harpoons and winches to lock the gondola in place, then, one by one, moved the mooring posts to the new location and made the balloon itself fast. Then Dieter dug out more posts from the storage crates, and released more lines that Lafayette hadn't even noticed tucked against the sides of the balloon before. These lines were attached to higher positions on the balloon itself, and once they were moored, then airship looked like a blobby sort of animal squatting low, as if hoping not to be noticed.

It was the best they could do against the storm that was still darkening the skies to the south. If they had been near any kind of hangar, they could've deflated the balloon and stored the entire thing far more securely. But they weren't near a hangar. They had no source to replace any gas they released now. So the balloon had to stay as it was.

Which was very vulnerable to damage. Lafayette didn't need to see the worried crease to Dieter's brow to know how vulnerable it was. She had felt its walls. They were still in good shape even after their long journey, but one moderately strong ice storm would be all it took to start punching the metallic fabric full of holes.

They had been briskly moving the entire time they were out in the night air, but even all that exercise hadn't been enough to keep the cold from seeping in to bite at her fingers and toes. She could feel a numbness that was growing into an ache, and when Dieter finally signaled that they should all slide back down the hole, Lafayette was immensely relieved.

Because before they had started moving the balloon, they had set up a camp of sorts down in the cavern. And Kora had been keeping an eye on things, because she couldn't really help with the airship, and even the warm clothes that Dieter had crafted for her still had too many gaps in them to keep her warm for long.

Not that it was much warmer down in the ice cavern than it had been on the surface. But the cooker was all set up, and it only took a few moments to get enough water boiling for them all to have coffee and rehydrated soup. Not a particularly filling meal—the soup was little more than broth with bits of onion floating in it—but the warmth of it in her belly quickly spread to the rest of her body.

Lafayette was pretty sure she wasn't going to lose any fingers or toes. Her hands had looked fine when she'd traded her heavy mittens for a lighter pair of gloves that she could actually grasp a mug in. And when she pulled off her boots to crawl inside her bedroll, her toes inside her thick socks felt alive when she wiggled them.

But what she wouldn't give for a long soak in a hot tub of water.

Tristan spread his own bedroll close beside hers, but Dieter left his folded up, merely moving it closer to the bottom of the ice tunnel and sitting on it with his back against one of the food crates they had carried down.

"Aren't you going to get some sleep?" Lafayette asked him, suddenly feeling guilty for already being tucked up snugly inside her own warm fur-lined bag.

"You two go ahead," Dieter said with a vague gesture. "I'll keep an eye on things."

"Why?" Tristan asked as he struggled to get his own boots off. "I mean, if the storm hits, what could you do? You can't go up there, even if something is happening."

"Look, I can't sleep, anyway. Leave me be," Dieter said.

"I'll sit up with you," Kora announced and padded over to lie beside him. She put her head on the knee of one of his crossed legs and looked up at him with her doggy eyes. "I can get up and down the tunnel more easily than any of you if something needs to be checked. And I require very little sleep."

Lafayette wasn't sure if that was, strictly speaking, true. Certainly, Kora seemed to engage in the act of sleeping more than any of the humans did. But it felt unkind to point it out now. Kora was probably still feeling like she wasn't much use, because as a dog she hadn't been able to help with anything on the airship. Keeping watch, though. That was totally something a dog could do.

"Wake us if you need us," Tristan said as he climbed into his bedroll.

"Sure thing," Dieter said. Then added, "Does the light bother you?"

While Kora had dimmed her indicator light, removing the eerie green glow from the cavern, the three lanterns they had carried down with them were all still emitting a soft yellowish light. It seemed to flicker over the ice like a cold sort of firelight.

"I don't mind it," Lafayette said.

"No, it's fine," Tristan said in a sleepy murmur.

Lafayette, who had been lying on her side while talking to Dieter and Kora, turned over to find Tristan closer beside her than she had thought. Not that they were remotely touching. Both of them were still in their parkas as well as everything else but their boots, and the bedrolls themselves were quite thick.

But he was close enough for her to feel the warmth of his breath on her face, and she was sure he felt hers too. And that felt cozy in a way she couldn't quite describe.

"We start digging in the morning," Tristan mumbled, his eyes already closed. "Or whenever we get up."

"Yes," Lafayette agreed.

But in the morning, they'd also start their first day of half rations. And while the soup had warmed her up, it had left her feeling hungrier than she'd been before she'd eaten it.

She had been hungrier than this in the past, and she knew it was manageable. She just didn't know how long it would remain manageable. How would she feel this time tomorrow? Or the day after that?

But she was so exhausted, even those worries couldn't keep her awake.

Her dreams were filled with the sound of wind, but when she woke, the only sound she heard was the soft murmur of voices. Kora and Dieter, talking. She had tucked her face down inside her bedroll at some point, so now she had to claw her way out of the bag and push the hood back out of her eyes.

The cavern looked exactly like it had the moment she had drifted off to sleep, even down to Dieter sitting cross-legged with Kora's head resting on his knee. She felt like her dreams of wind had carried on for hours and hours, but had any time passed at all?

"Is it storming?" she asked softly.

"I'm awake," Tristan mumbled from behind her. "Kind of."

"No storm yet," Dieter said. "We have one last serving of oatmeal for each of us. Then it's nothing but the soups and stews we've all been avoiding since we left the capital."

"But there's more than enough coffee," Kora piped up.

"Yeah, my sisters really erred on the side of caution with the caffeine supply," Dieter said with a fond chuckle.

"So we'll be warm on the inside and fully caffeinated, anyway," Lafayette said with as much upbeat attitude as she could muster so early in the morning.

Or at least she assumed it was early in the morning. Clearly, time of day in a cavern far below the surface of the ice was largely academic.

"Food, then digging," Tristan said as he slapped his mittened hands together. He was already standing up in his boots, ready for the day. Lafayette squirmed out of her own bag and fumbled to do the same.

They ate as slowly as they could bear to, making every bite of sweet oatmeal last as long as it possibly could. Then Dieter led them to the narrow end of the cavern.

"Kora helped me make some measurements while you guys were sleeping," Dieter said, destroying the illusion that Lafayette had formed in her mind of everything remaining frozen in place while she had slept. Apparently, the two of them had been quite busy, if quietly so.

"I can see through the ice slightly better than you can," Kora said, sounding almost apologetic. "I'm quite certain I see a doorway."

"Yes, I thought so too," Lafayette readily agreed. "An airlock, like where we escaped from those cat things when we were following my dad's trail."

"Yes, exactly," Kora said. "It's just a little bit lower than our elevation here, but it's further south and a bit to the east."

"I think I see it," Tristan said from where he was standing with nothing but his parka hood and hat between his forehead and the ice. He cupped his hands around his eyes to shut out the glare from the lantern light. "I *think* I do."

"I marked where we should start tunneling," Dieter said, showing them where he had staked out a section of ice using bits of metal as stakes and used a length of knitting yarn to define the perimeter. Part of that staked out space was on the floor of the cavern, but most of it was running up one of the irregular icy walls. "It's going to slope down, but only gradually. I was tempted to start working the space with a pickaxe, especially when neither of you so much as stirred when I pounded the stakes in, but Kora persuaded me to wait."

"Thank you," Lafayette said to both of them. "Can we all work on this at once?"

"Not really," Dieter said, sounding almost merry at that assessment. "In fact, one person at a time might be the only way to go, especially if we don't want to try for a bigger tunnel than we absolutely need."

"That's okay," Tristan said. "I mean, this is already going to be exhausting work. We should rotate work and rest, so at least one of us is always making progress. That seems the most efficient."

"So we're back to a schedule," Lafayette said. She tried really hard not to let her disappointment in that necessary fact show. But she couldn't argue with his point. It *would* be the most efficient use of their precious remaining time.

"Not eight hours of tunneling at a time, though," Dieter said. "That's too much. Look, I'm going to crash now, let's say for eight hours of sleep. You two can take turns swinging the pickaxe for as long as you can before switching out. Then, in eight hours when I get up, I'll switch places with one of you."

"Sixteen hours of tunneling, then?" Tristan said with a frown.

"Well, tunneling or watching the tunneling," Dieter said. "We're going to want someone awake and watching in case things go sideways."

"Sure," Tristan said.

"It's not like those lanterns are bright enough for us to carry on with our journaling work," Lafayette pointed out. "And it's too cold to go long with only thin gloves on. I don't know about you, but I can't really write legibly with my mittens on."

"I can't even feed myself with my mittens on," Tristan said with a grin.

"Bed," Dieter announced. "Wake me if you need me."

"We're going to be making noise," Tristan said with a wince, but Dieter just waved his words away.

"I'm dead tired. It won't matter."

As much as he wanted the two of them to believe he was preparing for eight hours of deep, uninterrupted sleep, Lafayette wasn't fooled. He didn't move his bedroll from where he'd been sitting on it, at the bottom of the tunnel. He just kicked it open and crawled inside.

She knew he was still listening for the sounds of a storm on the surface. He might doze a little, but he wasn't going to get anything like the sleep she and Tristan had just had.

"He's going to burn out on us," Lafayette said as Tristan adjusted his mittened grip on the closest of the pickaxes.

"He's worried about his family's ship," Tristan said.

"Which he's going to have to be awake enough to fly when this storm passes, right?" Lafayette pressed.

Tristan chewed at his lip. "Look, let him do what he needs to do now. Give it a couple of days. Then, if he's still pushing himself too hard, I'll talk to him."

Lafayette wanted to argue, but she just nodded. Tristan had known Dieter longer than she had. He knew Dieter's limits. But more than that, if one of them were going to talk to Dieter about staying within his limits, it kind of had to be Tristan.

Although Lafayette couldn't help but notice that Kora had snuggled down inside Dieter's bedroll to curl up against his parka'd belly. Just like she had always done with Lafayette before.

Kora was working hard to bond with Dieter. And Dieter was accepting her readily. Maybe, if the time came when they had to sit Dieter down and explain how much they needed him to take better care of himself, Kora would be the one who could better speak his language.

But Tristan wasn't wrong. That decision was still some days in their future.

In the meantime, they had a lot of tunneling through ice to do.

Tristan, finally satisfied with his grip on the handle, swung the pickaxe in an arc and brought the tip of it down. He sent only a single chip of ice flying out of the zone that Dieter had staked out.

But it was the first chip of ice. It was where they were starting.

He brought the axe up high and swung again.

CHAPTER 14

t was really hard to keep swinging a pickaxe against a wall of ice all day when all you were fueling yourself with was gritty coffee and a variety of soups that were little more than broth with various paltry floating bits. The different "flavors" meant different paltry floating bits. It was all almost irritatingly disappointing.

Even the stew was just broth with floating bits. Lafayette wanted to have words with whoever packaged these products. Because soup and stew weren't meant to be two words for the same thing.

And, frankly, neither of those words should be used to label the contents she was attempting to subsist on at the moment. Just name it chunky hot water, where you provided the hot water, and call it a day.

Yeah, Lafayette's boundless optimism was definitely going through a dark phase. But after so many days of hard work on few calories, she felt that was only appropriate. At least Dieter had eased up on his relentless vigilance. Or the exhaustion of life in the cavern made sleep impossible to avoid.

On the plus side, they had nearly reached their target: the airlock doorway.

On the minus side, they were so close that none of them felt like swinging the pickaxes anymore was a good idea. They were too likely to damage something. And, given the relative thickness of the hulls on these spaceships, Lafayette was pretty sure the thing they'd be damaging was themselves.

They were all tired, cranky, and hungry. Adding an injury to any of them to that list would spell disaster.

So now they were working with smaller tools like hammers and chisels. Which made the work go even more slowly.

But, on the other hand, there was no longer any reason to spot each other and switch positions so frequently. Which was a good thing.

Because as much as they had so much more space here than they had had back on the gondola, it still felt like far too cramped of quarters to share with two other humans who were increasingly getting on her nerves.

And she knew they felt the same. They were all clearly fighting the urge to snap at each other every time any of them spoke up.

So, yeah, Lafayette didn't mind being alone in the tunnel, lying on her back with one of the lanterns positioned just over her shoulder as she chipped away at the top of the ice tunnel. She was slowly working her way ever closer to what she knew was the panel to open the door.

The completely inert panel. None of the indicator lights was even dimly illuminated. She was pretty sure that when she finally broke away the last of the ice and could touch those buttons, absolutely nothing was going to happen.

But that was okay. It was Dieter's and Tristan's job to clear the ice away from the door itself. And if they had to, once that was clear, Lafayette knew they could force their way inside.

It's what her father had done, what felt like a lifetime ago in a much warmer place.

At least here there were no jungle animals stalking her every step. The Arctic waste had that going for it.

"Time," she heard Tristan call from the far end of the tunnel. Just the one word, and that almost grudgingly. She didn't call back, but he didn't need her to. He knew she had heard him.

She tucked her tools into the pockets of her parka, making sure they were secure. Then, leaving the lantern just where it was, she started sliding bit by bit back out of the tunnel, digging into the icy floor with the heels of her boots and dragging herself out into the cavern.

Tristan was waiting for her to emerge, hammer in hand. He gave her a nod as they changed places. He squirmed into the tunnel on his belly, quickly slipping out of sight.

Dieter was curled up inside his bedroll, as always just at the bottom of the tunnel that led up to the surface. The still storm-free surface. Lafayette almost wondered if the constantly building, never breaking storm was part of what was making life so tense down in the cavern. But really, did they need another reason? They had so many already.

Lafayette filled the kettle and sat down to watch it come to a boil. They had all agreed this step was necessary, as while they still had plenty of water, the cooking fuel was running precariously low. So she just sat and watched the kettle, snapping off the burner the instant the kettle started to bubble. No need to wait until it whistled; she knew it was hot enough, and every second of fuel use mattered.

They were so close, though. So close to getting inside that ship. So close to having access to heat and proper food and so much space. She didn't need another entire eight-hour shift to get that panel free. And she knew that Dieter and Tristan between them were very close to uncovering the door itself.

But somehow, knowing how close they were to better things just made the gritty coffee and watery soup that much more unsatisfying. She didn't even bother glancing at the label on the soup to see which floating bits she was getting this time. They were all pretty much the same. She just got it all down as fast as she could, because feeling that warmth in her belly was the highlight of her day.

Then she crawled inside her bedroll and tried to get to sleep. If she managed it before the warmth of her meal dissipated, she might get a few good hours of rest in. But if she didn't, if that warmth faded before she was in dreamland, then the hunger pangs would start. And then there'd be no sleep at all. Not for her.

She was just drifting off when she felt Kora's nose press against her cheek. Kora didn't speak. She alone among them was getting more than enough food, although her nutritive paste was so specific to her needs that there was no point in any of the rest of them even trying it.

It wasn't food for humans. Still, Kora respected that everyone else was having a tough time of it. And that silence was their only response to it all.

But she didn't need to speak for Lafayette to know what she wanted. She just lifted the edge of the bedroll and held it high enough for the dog to squirm inside. Then she laboriously turned around, the confines of the bag almost too tight for her to manage it. But then she succeeded and flopped down with a humph, pressing the length of her body against Lafayette's belly.

Lafayette draped an arm around the dog's metallic middle, then drifted back to sleep.

She woke up groggy an uncertain amount of time later. Dieter and Tristan were both awake, chattering loudly, but it was like Lafayette's brain was no longer capable of making sense of those sounds. They must be words. But she was too fuzzy-brained at first to even grasp the tone of their voices.

Then she did. They were excited. Excited in a good way.

"What's going on?" Lafayette asked as she climbed out of her bedroll. Kora was no longer with her. How long had she slept? She had no idea. It was like time didn't exist at all in this space with no access to the sun, moons or stars.

"You said a pry bar would do it, right?" Dieter said, rushing towards her. Too loud, too aggressive. No, still just excited. But it was a lot.

Lafayette's stomach growled in complaint. But she ignored it.

"The door?" Lafayette guessed as she reached for her boots. "There's a notch—"

"Yes, I saw it," Dieter said. "We can force our way in. That panel of yours isn't looking like it will even work, so we might as well just force our way in."

"It's not easy," Lafayette said.

"Pry bar!" Tristan called from the far side of the cavern where he was digging through the crates they had brought down from the gondola.

"I've got it," Dieter said, snatching the tool from him and diving headfirst into the tunnel.

Then Tristan went in after him.

Which was maddening. Because even if Lafayette followed, all she would be able to see was the bottoms of Tristan's boots. The space inside was simply too tight.

Well, they'd just have to come tell her if they got inside. She moved over to the cooker and put water in the kettle. It wasn't time for her food ration yet, but coffee was always available. And at least it was something. The gritty texture was almost a highlight now. It gave her something to chew, if only briefly.

She was still watching for the kettle to boil when Kora emerged from the tunnel. Which gave Lafayette a start. Dieter had gone in first, then Tristan. Lafayette hadn't seen Kora at all before then, so she must've already been inside the tunnel. But then, how had she gotten out? There'd have been two large bodies in her way with Dieter and Tristan inside.

"Lafayette!" Kora cried as she trotted over. "We're nearly there!"

"So I heard," Lafayette said. "How did that happen so fast? Or was I just asleep for that long? In which case, I can eat again."

"You slept for seven hours," Kora told her. "So no food yet. But Tristan broke through about an hour ago. The space around the doorway was a bubble in the ice, and once he broke through the wall of that bubble, it's just been clearing away the fragments to get to the door."

"Wow. I didn't even see that," Lafayette said. Not that she'd spent a lot of time examining the door area. The panel had been her assigned task. Still, an air bubble in the ice? It felt like she should've noticed that. Or someone should have.

The water in the kettle was nearly boiling, so she switched off the burner then poured it into her mug filled with coffee powder. She stirred it carefully with a spoon, for all the good that ever did. It would still be gritty.

But she looked down at Kora. "It's the same size as the one we were in before, right?" she asked. "Room enough for you and me and two or three jungle cats?"

"Yes," Kora said. "Or you and me and Tristan and Dieter. Who are currently taking turns with the pry bar."

"I told them it wouldn't be easy," Lafayette said as she downed her coffee in three swallows. Not that she knew exactly how much work it was. All she had done was reopen a door her father had broken into. The real work had been his.

"The panel is inert," she said to Kora as she cleaned the mug then set it back with the others on the crate they were using as a makeshift countertop. "What does that mean for the rest of the ship?"

"I don't know," Kora admitted. "We'll just have to see how things look once we're inside. Aren't you coming?"

"Yes, let's go," Lafayette said. Kora led the way through the narrow tunnel. With the dog's body between her and the lantern at the far end, and her own body between her and the light coming from behind her, it was completely dark, but she was used to that by now. The tunnel only went in one direction. It wasn't like she was going to get lost.

Then all at once Kora was out of the way, and Lafayette had the glow from that lantern blasting her full in the face. She blinked as she squirmed out of the tunnel and into the air pocket.

She felt a hand on her parka sleeve. It was Tristan, not so much helping her up as being sure she stood up far enough away not to interfere with Dieter, who was straining at the pry bar they had jammed between the door and the frame.

"It's moving," Dieter said between gritted teeth. "It's like it's on a track that's fighting me, but I can feel it giving bit by bit."

"Do you want me to take a turn?" Tristan offered.

But before Dieter could even answer, there was a loud squeal of metal against metal. It echoed through the air pocket, painfully loud even through the layers of hat and parka hood they all were sporting.

Then there was a boom, and Dieter was stumbling back into Tristan and Lafayette, pry bar flying. They all ducked instinctively until that metal implement had clattered to the icy ground.

And then all was silent. But it was a big silence. It was a silence that was echoing through a very large space.

And the three of them were staring into the deep black rectangle that was the doorway in front of them, leading into darkness.

CHAPTER 15

As anxious as she had been to find a way inside of this spaceship, Lafayette found herself frozen in place, unable to move forward through the open door.

Granted, it was an open door into bone-chillingly cold pitch blackness. A complete darkness that felt immense, because it was.

It felt like it was waiting to swallow her up.

But then she felt Kora brushing past her, trotting forward as she sniffed at the air with her doggy nose.

"Kora," Lafayette said, not quite restraining the dog but fighting the urge to do so. "There's no barrier before the drop-off, remember?"

"I know," Kora told her, still snuffling the stale-smelling air.

"What's this now?" Dieter asked, reaching for the closest of the lanterns. It was like the darkness beyond just wicked all that light away the instant it came in contact with it. It glowed like the dimmest of stars, illuminating nothing save the features of Dieter's own face. "It's not any warmer in here."

"No, it won't be until we get the power on," Lafayette said.

"We've come in at the wheel section of the ship," Tristan said, but musingly. As if he were still thinking it all through himself even as he pictured it. "In space, this wheel turns fast enough to simulate gravity, so 'down' when it's moving properly would be to the outer edges of the wheel. Where we are now—this airlock—would come up out of the floor under normal circumstances."

"I don't think they used these much when the station was under spin," Lafayette said. "There are larger hatches in the central core of the ship, which doesn't spin."

"Which is where engineering and everything else important is," Dieter said. "So that's where we're heading. But how do we get there? We're not coming up out of a floor now. We're moving sideways. To, apparently, a drop-off."

"We're going to need the rope," Tristan said.

"Lafayette can climb without a rope," Kora said proudly. "She did it before."

"Yes, but it's safer with rope as a tether," Lafayette said.

"I'll get it," Dieter said.

"I'm going to grab my bag as well," Tristan said.

Lafayette realized that she, too, wanted her bag with her. So all three of them plus Kora crawled back through the tiny tunnel through the ice to the cavern that had been their makeshift home for so many days. Lafayette checked that all of her journals were in the bag, plus writing utensils, a couple of bottles of water, and her pocket tool. She would normally pack some kind of snack, but she could already see Dieter shoving the last of their food supplies into his own bag, so she settled for just bringing a couple of tubes of Kora's nutritional paste.

Tristan moved around the cavern, making sure everything was stowed as it should be and that the stove wasn't running for some reason. Then, without a word, the three of them went back through to the airlock, Kora close at Lafayette's heels.

"I can climb first, if you like," Lafayette volunteered. "It's pretty dark, but I remember the layout well enough not to get disoriented. Then I can secure a rope for the two of you to follow."

"Here," Tristan said, and Lafayette turned just as he looped something over her head in its hat and parka hood. He had tied a length of sturdy string to one of the lanterns so she could wear it around her neck. Then he took another length of the same string to run through a loop in the bottom of the lantern and then around her chest just under her armpits. "So it doesn't swing around on you," he said.

"Thanks," she said, touching the light with one gloved hand. It still looked so dim, almost useless. But she was sure her eyes would adjust soon enough.

She was a little worried about her hands. The gloves were thick, but not as thick as her mittens. But the mittens would be useless for trying to climb in, at least until she reached far enough up the slope to where she was mostly walking stooped over with her hands just for guidance.

But she was going to be touching a lot of metal, metal so cold it would adhere to and cold-burn any exposed flesh. She hoped the gloves would be thick enough to hold that chill at bay.

"I'll be with you the whole way," Kora announced as Lafayette edged closer into the darkness beyond the open doorway. "Shall I carry a second rope?"

"That's not a bad idea," Dieter said, and quickly ran a rope around her midsection, fastening it securely in one of his strongest knots.

Then Lafayette gave Dieter and Tristan one last nod before turning her attention to the darkness. She shuffled to the edge of the airlock. There wasn't any kind of breeze in that corridor, and yet something about the air felt different as it moved past her face. Lafayette stopped with her toes just at the edge, then felt around the wall above her until her fingers caught at the metal lip of the airlock opening. She grasped it firmly and then hoisted herself up onto the narrow ledge of the doorframe.

She was standing pressed against the rough carpeting of the floor. The ceiling she knew was only a couple of meters opposite her was lost to darkness. She barely had room to stand on the airlock lip, and shuffling along it was terrifying. She had no handholds, nothing to catch herself with if she stumbled.

But then she felt the wall press against her shoulder, and she tentatively reached out a hand, groping for the side of a doorframe she knew would be there somewhere.

The instant her hand caught it, everything became much easier in her mind. The rooms in the wheel section were long and narrow, which meant the doorways were close together. It was a lot of stretching and hoisting, but there was a rhythm to it.

And so she was climbing, doorway to doorway through the darkness that still refused to let her vision penetrate it. Kora floated close beside her as if ready to catch her if she slipped, although Lafayette honestly didn't know if that would do any good. Dieter was below her, feeding out his end of the line that was also fastened to the back of the belt that Lafayette had fastened outside her parka. He, too, would probably try to catch her if she fell. But that just felt like a situation where all of them would end up getting hurt.

The only thing to do was to be sure she didn't fall.

It felt like she'd been climbing forever on an infinite loop, going from doorway to doorway but always the same two doorways. But slowly she realized that she was making out more details of the world around her, although the lantern around her neck hadn't gotten any brighter.

"I believe you're nearly out of rope," Kora said, glancing down between her own dangling paws at the airlock somewhere far below them. "I am too. I can feel the tension changing."

"Can you still see Dieter and Tristan?" Lafayette asked. She had taken a brief break in her climbing, but she was very reluctant to try looking down.

"No, they're too far past the curvature," Kora said.

Lafayette was a little surprised to hear that. As much as it felt like she'd been climbing for hours and hours, it hadn't felt like the angle of the corridor had changed at all. But now that Kora was mentioning it, she realized it had. It was no longer truly vertical. It was curving in, although not enough to be a walkable slope just yet.

"I'm going to open this door," Lafayette decided, reaching for the pry bar in the bag she had slung on her back and fitting the end of it just where the door met the frame. This door opened far more readily than the airlock had, sliding down with only minimal pushing from Lafayette's already weary arms.

The space inside was tiny. It ran deep enough to accommodate the four bunks built into its walls, but there was only the narrowest of spaces between the bunks. The bunks themselves were clearly only for sleeping in. Anyone larger than a child would find it quite impossible to sit up in one.

But there were rungs built into the walls near the doorway to assist in getting to the top bunks. Lafayette tied off first her rope and then Kora's, and then shouted back down the way they'd come.

"Come on up!"

No one answered her. But then the ropes first danced about and then snapped tight, and she knew the two of them were on their way up to her and Kora.

"Shall we wait here or carry on?" Kora asked her.

But Lafayette was already searching the room for anything of interest. The bunks were contoured out of the walls themselves, not separate pieces of furniture, and they had been stripped of mattresses and bedding entirely. There were a few drawers built into the space above and below the bunks, drawers that opened readily at the softest of touches. But they, too, were bare.

"They stripped this place," Lafayette said. "They took what they needed when they walked away."

"My ship too had been stripped down," Kora reminded her.

"The wheel section was," Lafayette said. "There were still supplies in the core."

"Perhaps that will be true here as well," Kora said. "We haven't reached the core yet."

"Yeah," Lafayette said, then sighed. "We should've brought more rope."

"We can pull up and reuse the other ropes once Dieter and Tristan get here," Kora said.

"No," Lafayette said. "We should leave those where they are. In case we have to get out of here in a hurry."

Like she had done, leaving the other ship. That had been a harrowing journey, climbing down the steep corridor. Trying to both escape before the ship either launched or exploded, but also trying very hard not to trip and fall.

"We should keep climbing," Lafayette decided at last. "I don't think we'll have to go much further to get to the nearest spoke in to the core. We've come so far already."

"I agree; we must be close," Kora said. "I can look ahead?"

"No, I'm coming too," Lafayette said. Then she slapped her hands together before resuming her climb from doorway to doorway.

She only had to go three more doorways before she reached the spoke she was looking for. Only, of course, because she knew somewhere in her head that it had to be, the opening into that spoke was nowhere near a climbable doorway.

And while the floor to her right was gaining an almost climbable slope to it, the spoke opened up out of the ceiling. Which wasn't.

"I can jump it," Lafayette said even as she struggled to open another doorway on her side of the corridor first, to give her more space to jump from.

"Are you sure?" Kora asked with deep worry.

"Yeah, it's not far," Lafayette said. "I just need to get a run-up."

She could hear the sounds of Dieter and Tristan not far below her now, but she didn't wait to confer with either of them first. She just backed up to the far side of the room lined with bunks identical to the other, then started running. The ledge between the two bunks that lined the wall that was currently her floor was just barely wide enough for her booted feet to even fit on, but her steps were sure. She reached the very end of the room and then jumped, sailing up into the air.

For a moment, it was like she was weightless.

Then gravity reasserted itself, and she was falling. She knew even in the darkness that she was short of her mark, but she threw her upper body forward, catching with her arms what her feet were missing. The edge of the spoke corridor.

That edge caught her in the stomach, knocking the air out of her. Then she started to slide, but only for a moment. Because Kora was there with her, catching the top of the hood of her parka firmly in her teeth before reversing her hover disk. Kora was now a complete deadweight, one that was not going to let Lafayette fall.

"Are you insane?" Dieter was calling up to her. "I have more rope."

"Wouldn't have helped," Lafayette grunted, her breath still coming in spasms. But slowly she got her hands under her and crawled up to safety.

"I'll fetch the rope," Kora said once Lafayette was sitting on firm ground. She hovered out into the center of the bottomless corridor and then lowered like an elevator down to the room where Dieter and Tristan were gathered.

She came up again seconds later with a new line tethered to her midsection. Lafayette examined the knot briefly, saw the end of it dangling in an obvious way out of the knot and gave it a tug. The rope pulled free from Kora's middle with ease, and Lafayette took a moment to find the nearest bit of locked-down architecture she could tie it to.

It was only after the knot was secure and she'd called down to the others that Lafayette realized where she was standing. The floor of the spoke corridor was currently a wall, so the niche she was standing in had once been built into the wall of the corridor. Still, Lafayette recognized the space at once. She had seen similar niches on the other ship.

Although all of those niches had contained security robots, like the ones that had come to life and dragged her father off to the brig after he had accidentally triggered something in the engineering room.

So, was the lack of robots now a good thing, since it was one less danger for them to deal with?

Or was it a bad thing? Because if the occupants of the ship had taken even the robots out of the ship, maybe there was nothing left for Lafayette and her friends to use. Maybe this whole thing was nothing more than an oversized lump of useless metal.

Lafayette chewed at her lip, but decided to keep her fears to herself for now. They would all know soon enough whether this entire journey had been pointless or not. In the meantime, she'd keep everyone moving in the right direction for as long as she could.

She turned to help Dieter and Tristan get over the lip of the corridor's end.

CHAPTER 16

The corridor that followed the spoke of the wheel ran downhill pretty steeply, but once it reached the core everything became almost level. The ship had crashed not only nose-down, but almost exactly balanced on that nose. Which meant that all the parts of the ship where acceleration—or, as in the case of these ships, which had been approaching their final destination, deceleration—had provided the sensation of gravity were aligned correctly with the planetary gravity.

A coincidence, surely, but a convenient one. It meant, once they left the spoke behind, they could walk through corridors and rooms that were the right way up.

Sadly, unlike in the other ship, there were no emergency lights running anywhere. Everything was still ice-cold and dark. The layout was the same as the ship her father was on, so Lafayette easily found the brig, more niches where security robots should be docked, and even the classrooms.

But the classrooms, like the bunk rooms in the wheel, had been stripped of everything. The shelves were bare. The desks in the front of the rooms had open sockets where the learning construct drives should be slotted. And there wasn't a tablet or book to be found anywhere.

"This is terribly disappointing," Kora said with a sigh.

"Were you hoping to talk to another teacher?" Lafayette asked. "I'm sorry. As fixated as I am to get back to my father, I didn't even think how lonely you must be."

"I'm not lonely," Kora assured her. "I just would've liked to find at least one reader to use to teach Tristan. Perhaps I'll have to use that diary of yours after all."

"Well, let's not give up yet," Lafayette said, feeling that betraying rush of heat to her cheeks all over again. At least with her hood up and her scarf mostly covering her lower face, she doubted anyone else noticed.

Especially not in the persistent dark.

"Let's find engineering," Dieter suggested.

Lafayette led the way to the room at the center of the ship's core. It ran for more levels than Lafayette had ever tried to count, above and below the level they were on, but most of the controls were where they were.

But those controls were as inert as anything else. Lafayette pressed button after button, but nothing responded to her touch.

"Life support systems," Kora said from the far end of the room. "Look, this is what we need to start with. Heat, food and water."

"All out of that console there?" Dieter asked skeptically. It was just a panel with dials and blank readouts on it. A little fancier than the cockpit of his family's airship, but not by much.

"Look, the engine isn't entirely drained," Kora said, trotting from the console she had just pointed out to the center of the room. "You can see the light still being emitted from it."

Lafayette wasn't sure at first if she agreed that was true. She couldn't see anything like a source of light anywhere.

And yet, it was easier to see the others as they moved through the dark, shining their lanterns into every nook and cranny. There *was* more ambient light, if only just.

"The life support systems are designed to work when all else fails," Kora insisted, trotting back to the console. Lafayette followed her, but pushing buttons on that panel did no more than any of the others.

"Oh," Dieter said in sudden understanding. "I think she's right. Look, there's a manual set of switches back here."

He was standing off to Lafayette's left, shining his lantern at something she couldn't see on the side of the console she was examining. Tristan came up behind him and was quickly nodding his agreement.

"Yes, that's it," Kora said. "It has to be."

"You're sure?" Tristan asked. "I thought you were never in engineering until Lafayette brought you there."

"That's true, but I have some knowledge of how things work," Kora said. "Not a lot, granted. And it's pretty basic, what I know."

"It's from novels and entertainments," Dieter said, and Lafayette could hear the smirk in his voice.

"It's true," Kora admitted.

"Yeah, she told me as much when we were going over the airship controls together," Dieter said. "So this only works if the writers of those entertainments cared about the details."

"Maybe I should try reading the labels," Lafayette offered.

"No point," Tristan said. "There aren't any."

"Look, if nothing happens when I throw all these switches, it's not like we're any worse off," Dieter said.

"But what if the wrong things happen?" Lafayette said.

Dieter just shrugged. Then, before she could say a word or make any movement to stop him, he leaned forward and swept his gloved hands up the whole line of switches.

Lafayette yelped in involuntary alarm. But then yelped again in something more like excitement when the lights flickered on, and she heard the sound of machines all around them humming back to life.

Heat. It would be warm soon. And the air recyclers would get to work on the stale smell too, she hoped.

But it was a big ship. It would take a while to warm up.

Luckily, she knew at least one thing that would work almost instantly.

"Come on," she said, tugging at Tristan's sleeve to get him to follow her.

"Where are we going?" he asked even as he matched her swift pace out of the engineering room.

"Back to the brig," she said, glancing back only long enough to see that Dieter, too, was following her. "I'm going to get us some proper food."

"The brig," Dieter said. "Isn't that like a jail or something?"

"It has beds and food," Lafayette told him. "If we don't turn on the security fields for the cells, we won't get locked in."

Perhaps not surprisingly, the bunks in the brig didn't have mattresses and bedding. But at least the food dispensers worked. Not that Lafayette could pick what they produced any more than her father ever had. But every time she pressed the button at the security officer's desk, the dispensers built into the cells produced another complete meal.

Lafayette pressed it three times in succession. Soon the four cells each had a breakfast of bacon, eggs, toast and coffee, then a lunch of sliced hot turkey and some kind of white cheese that was just starting to melt in a sandwich made of dark, crusty bread, and finally a dinner of noodles in a rich red sauce.

"This is tomato," Dieter said with surprise.

"What's a tomato?" Tristan asked as he took a bite. "I mean, aside from awesome. Because this is awesome."

"They grow them in some of the villages in the southwest quadrant," Dieter said between huge bites of food. "They don't travel well, so most caravans don't attempt to buy or sell them. But whenever my family was in the area, we always stuffed ourselves silly. This sauce is pretty good, but not the best I've tasted."

"After all that thin soup for days, you won't get a complaint out of me," Lafayette said.

Although, when the food was all gone, she was tempted to complain about the fullness of her belly.

"I was planning to go back to fetch more of our equipment, but I don't think I can even get up now," Dieter said, rubbing his own stomach in a satisfied manner.

"The morning," Tristan said groggily. "We can do it all in the morning. It'll be easier to climb when it's warm enough to ditch the gloves, anyway."

"Kora, do you think the other systems might start responding once the ship is warmer?" Lafayette asked.

"I don't know," Kora admitted. "Perhaps?"

"It looks like everything that wasn't built in was hauled away," Dieter said. "The ship in the center of the capital city had more left behind than this. Not that much of it was of any use besides that tablet. Still, the beds had blankets and sheets and stuff."

"Sure, but they'd been there for centuries," Tristan said.

There were four cells with bunks, food dispensers, and plumbing all tucked inside, and given the staggered layout of the doorways, once they were inside any of them, none of the others could see in without making a point of it. Still, eventually, if they ended up staying here for long, Lafayette was going to want at least a curtain across her doorway.

But not that night. No, this was another in a long series of nights where she knew she'd be sleeping in her parka. Only this time, she didn't think she'd even take her boots off.

She had a brief moment to lament how difficult it was going to be sleeping like this, and then she was out like a light.

She woke some time later to find the air only a little warmer. But it was filled again with the scent of bacon. Lafayette stretched her limbs out, then rolled stiffly out of her bunk to step out of her cell.

"Hey," Dieter said, meeting her just outside her doorway with a bowl of scrambled eggs generously mixed with diced bacon and bits of bell peppers of several different colors. She took it from him at once—no one had to ask her twice to eat anything that smelled so divine—but she couldn't suppress the quizzical look she sent his way.

"Every time I push the button, we get four servings," he said with a shrug. "That one's yours."

"Yeah, but I have one in my own cell, apparently," she said, looking back over her shoulder to confirm this was, indeed, true. "It even stays warm in there if I don't open the door."

"Consider it a peace offering," Dieter said.

"For what?" Lafayette asked. But he crossed his arms and refused to say a word until she had put a spoonful of the fluffy eggs into her mouth.

Oh, she could get used to this. Even her stomach was growling in a happy, about to be satisfied gurgle. A welcome change from the days of low, angry grumbling.

"For what?" she asked again, but with a bit more of a merely curious, not suspicious, intonation.

"I went through your stuff while you were sleeping," he said, and pointed to the security officer's desk. Her bag was open on one end of it, all of her journals spilling out over the remainder of the surface.

"Well, technically speaking, the whole point of me writing it all down is for everyone to make use of it," she said around a mouthful of egg.

"Tristan said you wouldn't mind," Dieter said, although she could hear the relief in his voice like he, Dieter, had suspected otherwise.

"Where is Tristan?" she asked.

"He went to get our bedrolls, with Kora," Dieter said. And Lafayette, belatedly, noticed that the dog wasn't there. "They did the math before even I got up. At the rate things are warming up in here, we have at least one more night that's going to be on the chilly side. And Kora was up all night nosing around for any hint of a blanket but came up empty."

"They had a lot of time to move out of this ship," Lafayette said. "I only wonder where they went? Did they have something like an airship or even a boat to get them off the ice?"

"Maybe we'll find out when things warm up enough to function again," Dieter said. "So far, it's just life support, though. And no sign of any more tablets."

"We need to find the bridge," Lafayette said, scraping the last bits of diced bell pepper out of the bottom of her bowl. "Not that I think there will be tablets there, but there should be some kind of ship's log, wouldn't you think?"

"Or at least a copy of one, if they took the proper one with them," Dieter said. "That's what an airship captain would do, anyway. Even in my family, where we don't want any information to fall into Central Planning hands if we can help it."

"Yeah," Lafayette agreed, remembering the cryptic text she had seen his family use. A log written like that would be all but indecipherable to Central Planning, she was sure.

She just hoped this ship hadn't had such a need for secrecy.

"I've studied the ship schematics you drew," he said, gesturing towards her journals. "The ones you copied from your dad. I think I know where to go, but I didn't want you to wake up with all of us gone."

"Thanks," Lafayette said.

"It took longer than I thought for the scent of bacon to carry into your bunk," he said with the smallest of upward tilts to just the corner of his mouth.

"You couldn't have been standing there all so long," she said. "The bowl was still warm when I took it from you."

"That one was," he said, his mouth now stretched wide into a proper grin.

It might not be warm enough to work without gloves on yet, but just being able to loosen their scarves a bit was already making a world of difference.

She hadn't realized before just how isolating it had been, not really seeing anyone's faces but Kora's for so many days. Well, lots of things about the last several days were better forgotten.

"Come on," she said, snatching up the journal she had yet to finish writing in yet as well as a pen, then leading the way out of the brig.

Time to see if anything in this ship was working yet.

CHAPTER 17

Lafayette and Dieter found the bridge of the ship easily enough, although it was a bit of a hike, being almost a dozen levels down from where they were on the brig level. The lights were still running, and the air was moving around, if not growing warmer as quickly as Lafayette would have liked. But none of the automated doors would open. So, as much as Lafayette knew the ship had lifts that would move them between levels, they still had to do it the old-fashioned way.

Which wasn't even a stairwell, like on the ship in the center of the capital city. There might *be* stairs somewhere, behind one of the many locked doors, but what they had access to were the ladders connecting all the various decks of the engineering room.

Lafayette's body was still sore and worn out from the climbing she had done the day before. And while she'd stuffed herself with food twice now, she knew it would take more than that before she felt her usual strong self again.

But Dieter seemed to feel the same, because even though he took the lead down ladder after ladder, he kept up a steady but slow pace, just plodding from rung to rung until they finally reached the bridge level.

The corridors on this level were wider than at the brig level, and the doors that lined the corridor were consistently pairs of double doors, as if the rooms beyond them were equally oversized.

Lafayette saw more niches in the walls where security robots should be docked, but like below they were all empty.

Then they reached the open doorway that led into the bridge. There were three separate decks that stepped down from the horseshoe-shaped topmost where they were standing as they came into the doorway down to the lowest level nestled inside the curve of that horseshoe. Each deck was lined on two sides with workstations, consoles with an array of buttons and screens whose functions Lafayette could only guess at.

Because everything inside the bridge was completely inert. The lights were on, filling the space with a warm, comforting glow. But all the screens were dark, and none of the buttons did a thing when she pressed them.

"This is a little more complicated than an airship," Dieter said drily, running his hands along the edges of the consoles with something like admiration. Although, unlike Lafayette, he didn't attempt pushing any of the buttons.

"According to my father's notes, everything here is connected to another area in the ship," Lafayette told him. "Like there's a workstation somewhere that just relays information from the engineering room and displays it. So the captain, who I guess sits in that central chair right there, can compile everything and make and execute decisions."

"So a lot more complicated than an airship," Dieter said.

"Well, it's just a matter of figuring out what we need to know, and which workstation can tell us those things," Lafayette said. "Assuming when the engine has been running a little longer that any of this wakes up."

"I don't see any more manual switches," Dieter said. "So either they never expected to be in a situation like this, or if they did expect it, they were sure that the manual switches we found would be enough."

"I hope so," Lafayette said. "I just wish something was labeled. I want to know which of these workstations is going to let us communicate with the other ship."

"Probably one of the ones on the middle level, flanking that captain's chair," Dieter said, leading the way down a short stairway to where he had been pointing. "Communications is pretty important. It would be close by, I should think."

They examined each of the workstations one by one, but nothing looked remotely promising. They were different arrangements of screens and buttons, but just the mere arrangement of things told neither of them anything.

"If there are no labels on the consoles, it's because when the screens are active there'd be no need for such things, right?" Dieter asked.

"I guess so," Lafayette said.

"Hey, guys," Tristan said as he and Kora appeared in the doorway above them. He sounded a little out of breath. "I thought I'd find you here."

"For all the good it's done us," Dieter said. But despite his frustrated tone, he didn't stop examining the consoles.

"You got our bedrolls?" Lafayette asked.

"Yeah, plus a bag of spare clothes for each of us for when it gets warmer in here. But I also have some news," he said. He sounded nervous, and Lafayette sensed this wasn't going to be good news. "The storm finally rolled in. Kora and I could hear it even down in the cavern. It sounds like a doozy."

Dieter looked up, his face pale and tight. But he didn't say a word. Not that he needed to. Lafayette and Tristan both knew he was worried about his family's airship.

"We're quite well protected here, down in the ice," Kora said. "And it will be warmer soon. We'll be quite comfortable, I should think, by this time tomorrow."

"We'll be safe to stay here indefinitely, if we need to," Tristan said. "I mean, your family knows where we were going, right? When we don't get back, they'll know where to start looking for us. And once the storm passes, we can figure out a way to keep a watch out for them. We'll be okay."

"Yeah," Dieter said, and tried but failed to muster up any kind of smile.

"We might not even need to wait for that," Lafayette said.

"What do you mean?" Tristan asked her.

"Well, looking around here, this ship seems way too complicated for us to fly. Only, the one my father was on took off by itself. There are systems to make it do that," Lafayette said.

"So we can be trapped in orbit too?" Dieter asked.

"Well, no," Lafayette said. "I only meant, if we worked at it, we could figure out a way to fly this thing straight to the capital. If we wanted to. So maybe your family wouldn't have to put themselves in danger coming to get us."

"That's a lot of ifs," Dieter said.

"But we can keep it in mind as an option," Tristan said. "Didn't these massive ships have smaller launches too? To carry smaller numbers of people around on shorter journeys?"

"I think so," Lafayette said. Although she was fairly certain that, like the security robots and the blankets and everything else that wasn't bolted down, they would find the berths for those smaller ships quite empty.

Dieter just chewed his lip, looking down at the console he was standing over but with unfocused eyes. Then he lifted his head and started walking with purpose back up to the top deck, to another smaller doorway at one end of the top horseshoe.

"Where are you going?" Tristan asked even as he, Lafayette, and Kora moved to follow.

"There are living quarters this way on the schematics," Dieter said. The door at the end of the horseshoe was closed, and the panel beside it was darkly inert, but he didn't even try opening it that way. He just pulled his trusty pry bar out of his back pocket and slipped it into the notch that all the doors seemed to have for just this purpose.

It gave fairly easily, more like the doors to the living quarters in the wheel than the airlock door. Then they were in a narrower corridor than the others on this level. The lights were softer here, too, which made sense. If these living quarters were for the ship's officers, who would be working on various shift rotations, sleepy people would probably prefer not dealing with full-intensity lights in this private space.

The doors were smaller too; no double doors here. And they were equally spaced, two across from each other every dozen meters or so. Dieter stopped at the first pair, opening first one and then the other in quick succession before stowing his tool and walking into one of the rooms.

The space beyond was, by the standards of the other living quarters on the ship, immense. A single bed dominated one end of the room, a bed large enough to fit three or four people. The bedding was all gone, but the mattress remained. Given that the mattresses for the bunks in the other berths could be rolled up tight and carried around and this one was so thick Lafayette doubted it could even be folded at all, it wasn't surprising this got left behind.

Closer to the door than the bed, though, was a table and a pair of padded chairs. Like the furniture in the schoolrooms, these pieces looked like they grew up out of the floor like mushrooms, not so much bolted to the floor as one with it.

The other end of the room had an open doorway leading into a bathroom complete with a full-sized bathtub as well as a shower, sink, and toilet.

And on the wall beside that open door was a food replicator unit. Lafayette made a beeline for that, touching the panel before she could even work out how badly she wanted to see if it was working.

It whirred to life at once, the light inside glowing brightly and then fading away with a soft beep. Lafayette opened the door and took out the tray of prepared food. The contents of the bowl were a steaming puree, thick and red and smelling like the tomato sauce they had had the night before. Beside it was a plate of two rolls of crusty white bread and a pat of golden yellow butter.

"Right," Dieter said brightly as he helped himself to one of the rolls. "I assume we're all in agreement that we're moving down here?"

"Oh, sure," Tristan said as he took the other roll. "Just to be closer to the bridge, right?"

Lafayette picked up the spoon and dug into the soup. And here she'd thought she'd never willingly eat soup again. And yet this soup was so thick and creamy, even more intensely tomato-flavored than the sauce had been, but also with hints of basil, she was pretty sure she'd happily just eat this soup for days and days.

"If it's warmer tomorrow like Kora says it will be, maybe the other systems will start coming on line then," Lafayette said.

Dieter opened the next pair of doors, but each of the four rooms they now had access to was identical. They each picked one as their own, although Kora of course opted to stay with Lafayette in hers. Then they dialed up more soup and rolls for lunch.

They went back up all the ladders to the brig where they had left their stuff. It was awkward getting back down the ladders with her bag of journals, bag of clothes, and bedroll all dangling from straps over her shoulders, but it was manageable.

When they reached the corridor between the officers' living quarters once more, they all sort of hesitated awkwardly.

"There's really nothing we can do until tomorrow, right?" Tristan said.

"No, I don't think so," Dieter said. "And honestly, a little bit of time alone wouldn't be the worst thing in the world right now."

"Yeah, same," Tristan agreed.

"Thanks for thinking of the spare clothes, Tristan," Lafayette said. "I'm going to see if that tub works, and if it does, I'm going to take the hottest bath of my life before getting into clean clothes." Something she hadn't been able to do while they'd all been on top of each other down in the cavern. "I know I'll still have to get back into this parka after, but just something new against my skin is going to be so nice. Seriously, thanks so much."

Tristan mumbled something, his cheeks brightly red.

Dieter just grinned at him. "Yeah, thanks, man. What she said."

Tristan nodded at them both and then disappeared into his own room.

The water was indeed hot enough for Lafayette's tastes. And inside the confines of her bathroom with the door closed, the steam from the water warmed up the space enough that not even her exposed face and shoulders got cold. She soaked for what felt like hours, adding more hot water from time to time just for the pleasure of it.

By the time she had eaten a dinner of roasted chicken with potatoes and carrots and at least two other root vegetables she couldn't identify, she was more than ready to crawl back inside that bedroll.

In the morning, there would be tasks to do. But for now, she could just enjoy this: being well-fed, mostly warm, and almost entirely comfortable.

As she drifted off to sleep, she wondered if her father had explored the other parts of his own ship. With time, he must've found a way to get out of the brig on his ship. Maybe he, too, was soaking in warm baths and enjoying the comforts of an officer's quarters.

She'd like to think so.

But she'd really like to know for sure.

CHAPTER 18

Lafayette woke in what she assumed was the morning and used the replicator to summon another large meal. It was almost as if the ship knew she was still low in calories, providing her with an immense bowl of oatmeal surrounded by smaller bowls containing diced nuts, dried fruits, dark brown sugar and even a little pitcher of creamy milk. It looked like it would be too much for her when she took it out of the replicator, but Lafayette was surprised to find a few minutes later that she'd eaten it all.

The air was slowly getting warmer, if not quite comfortable yet. After getting out of her bedroll, Lafayette found she was comfortable without her scarf or hat. When she finished eating, she put on her thinnest pair of gloves, but with the warmth from the food and coffee in her stomach, she unzipped her parka and let it hang loosely around her, hood back.

It had been so many days since she'd been able to fluff out her hair buns. She thought the constant wearing of her hat and hood might've permanently squashed them down, but perhaps a night of sleeping without her parka on with the hood up would help. In the meantime, she fluffed them out to as spherical a state as she could manage, then headed out into the corridor towards the bridge, Kora close at her heels.

Tristan and Dieter were both already there, hovering around the console that Dieter was sure was the communications workstation. They were talking together in low voices, but they stopped when they heard her boots on the deck above them.

"Is it working?" Lafayette asked as she skipped down the stairway to the middle deck.

"Kind of," Tristan said. Like her, he was still wearing his parka, but unzipped and with the hood back. His reddish-blond hair looked recently washed, both curlier and longer than she remembered it being.

But, then again, it had been so long since they'd been able to see each other's faces for more than the briefest of moments. She hadn't realized just how much she had missed that. Looking into his eyes when he spoke to her and being able to really see them, with no tinted goggles in the way.

"I don't know if it's communications we're seeing," Dieter said, distracting Lafayette away from what she sensed was a too intense studying of Tristan's features. But he had been looking at her just as intently, making her grateful for the minutes she had just spent straightening up her own hair.

"What do you mean?" Lafayette asked, forcing her attention to focus on Dieter. Who, as it turned out, wasn't even wearing his parka. He had a thick flannel shirt on over his thermal undershirt, but even that he hadn't bothered to button up properly. Like the persisting cold didn't really bother him at all.

He touched a few of the screens with bare fingers. "It looks more like navigation information than communications," he said.

Lafayette frowned as she leaned in to see what he meant. He couldn't read the language, but as she got a closer look, she saw he didn't really need to. What they were looking at was clearly a slowly rotating three-dimensional map.

But not of the area around the ship. She didn't see the ice floe or the ocean or anything to indicate that.

No, it wasn't at that scale. It was much further out. Their position *was* marked on an ever so slightly curved surface.

"Right," Lafayette said, pointing with her own gloved fingers. "That's us. And that would make this dot over here the ship in the capital city."

Dieter sucked in a breath. "You're right," he said, as if angry at himself for not seeing that already.

"Isn't that what you meant?" Lafayette asked, confused.

"I knew it was *something*," he said. "Yeah, that's us. That's the capital city ship. But it's all pulled back from both because of this third point up in space." He threw her a sidelong glance. "I'm guessing that's your father."

"Right," Lafayette said. "And here, there's another point on the surface but far east and south of the capital city. That's got to be the ship that went down into the water."

"That's four," Tristan said even as he turned pages in the journal he was holding until he found his own version of the maps her father had drawn, the ones they had matched up to the information in the engineer's journal. He looked from his map to the rotating image and then back again. "Where's the fifth? It should be south of the capital city, in the mountains."

"Maybe it's too far south for this map," Dieter said. "Or the mountains are interfering somehow? Because this is coming in on some kind of signal, right? It knows your father's ship is up in space. I mean, if you watch it long enough, you can see the dot that marks your father's ship is moving."

"Kora?" Lafayette asked after watching the map long enough to see that Dieter was right. "Do you know anything about this?"

"Not really," Kora admitted, not quite hanging her doggy head but sounding like she wanted to. "I think you're right. That's a navigation workstation. So, I think the other one over there must be communications."

They all turned to look at the other workstation behind them, flanking the other side of the captain's chair.

Lafayette glanced at the other two, then walked over to look at the screens. There were readouts like patterns of wavy lines, and others like sequences of numbers. Neither of them meant anything to her.

Then she touched a button, and finally, finally, something happened when she did that.

They all heard voices, a sudden overlapping of voices pouring out of a speaker she only belatedly identified at the top of the console.

"I don't understand any of that," Tristan said after a moment.

"It's too many people all talking at once," Dieter said. "Can you make just one at a time play?"

"I don't know," Lafayette admitted. "Maybe? But even if I focus on just one voice at a time, none of it makes sense."

"It's not the language you learned from Kora?" Tristan asked.

"No, not remotely," Lafayette said.

"No, I don't understand any of those voices either," Kora said. "It's not just strange accents. It's at least one and maybe more languages I don't even speak."

"I think you're right, though," Lafayette said, looking at the array of buttons before her. Still without labels. "If I start fiddling with things, I think I can work out a way to listen to only one voice at a time. Maybe then it will make more sense."

She sat down in the chair and pulled out her journal. If she was going to be testing things, she would need to take copious notes of what worked and what didn't.

"I can try something similar with the navigation system," Tristan said. "It would be nice to see if we can get other maps, maybe maps more of the area immediately around the ship. I mean, if they really are showing us things as they are right now, there must be a way to see from here when the storm has passed. Right?"

"Stands to reason," Lafayette said. "It certainly can't hurt to try."

"Okay, but I have a question," Dieter said. "We're trapped under a great deal of ice. We can't see the surface, let alone get a sight line on the ship up in orbit or anything. So how does this ship know what's going on up there?"

"Oh, yes," Kora said, switching instantly to teacher mode. "I know your own communications systems work on line of sight. But while the starships in the fleet could easily also use line of sight for communications, we had a different way of staying in contact."

"What do you mean?" Lafayette asked.

"Well, we were so very far away from home," Kora said. "And we were very remote from the other fleets."

"The other fleets?" Tristan said, looking up from his own journal, hand poised in mid note-taking.

"Well, yes," Kora said. "We came to this planet looking to settle here, as you well know. But there were other fleets going to other planets. I thought you knew that as well?"

"Well, it makes sense," Dieter said.

"Yeah, but I never thought about it before," Tristan said, sounding awestruck.

"How many fleets?" Lafayette asked.

"I don't know," Kora admitted. "Thousands? But I think more."

"And you all stayed in contact with each other?" Dieter asked.

"Yes. Well, obviously something changed," Kora said. "We all crashed here, and no one ever came to help out. The ships are still here, and so are all of you descendants of the people who were on those ships. No one ever came, or you'd know about it. So something must have happened."

"More lost history," Tristan said.

"Okay," Dieter said. "But let's back up. How do the comms work?"

"I really don't know," Kora said. "I mean, I know there was something we called the systemic field that connected all ships. So that's why the map you're looking at now looks like it's projecting out from the ship in orbit and not this one. Because that ship is currently the core of the systemic field."

"Because it came back to life before this one did," Tristan guessed.

"Yes, I think so," Kora said. "Look, you all know I know most of this stuff from books I've read. Fiction, though. Not engineering books."

"So you know the fact that it exists but not anything about the how of it all," Dieter said.

"No. I know my students could send messages to other ships or even back to the home world, and they were received almost instantaneously. But that was just part of the world, not something I ever had to think about."

"It just worked like magic," Lafayette said.

"I mean, I knew it *wasn't* magic," Kora said.

"So these messages are coming in from all over the universe," Dieter said.

"I suppose so," Kora said.

"And yet you don't understand a word of it," he went on. "Can language really change that much?"

"Given how very long I was dormant in my classroom, I think so," Kora said. "Although I truly hope, if Lafayette can isolate the messages separately and I can really concentrate on the sounds, maybe it's like how I'm speaking to you now. This isn't the language I grew up speaking. But I can understand you now. Just as Lafayette can understand me when I speak in my own way."

"You should get on that, then, Lafayette," Dieter said.

"I was about to," she reminded him.

"And if Tristan can work out how to change the range on the navigation systems, maybe that will help us figure out the same thing with the communications," Dieter went on. "It would be nice to know which of those voices was coming from somewhere nearby and which ones weren't."

"I will assist Lafayette as much as I can," Kora announced, and curled up by Lafayette's ankles, resting her chin on the top of Lafayette's boot.

The first thing Lafayette worked out was how to turn down the volume from the speaker. Until she could isolate the messages, there was no reason to boom them loudly across the entire bridge.

After she did that, things grew very quiet save for the occasional clicking of a button followed by the scribbling of pen over paper as either Lafayette or Tristan behind her made notes.

For his part, Dieter moved from workstation to workstation all around all three decks of the bridge, studying the screens on each but never touching the buttons. He left briefly to fetch lunches for all of them so that she and Tristan didn't need to pause in their work for more than a quick stretch.

By the time Lafayette was ready to quit, call it a day and see what was for dinner, Dieter had stopped moving around. He was sitting, lost in deep thought, in the captain's chair.

It felt like his natural place. Not that she was going to say so out loud.

"I feel like I made some progress," she said as she got up and stretched up onto her tiptoes. She had taken off her parka at some point after lunch, but now even her sweater over her long underwear felt a touch too warm.

"Me too," Tristan said. "I think. I have some theories on what to try tomorrow, to get a closer map of the area around us."

"You were getting snowy images," Dieter said from where he was still sitting with his chin on his steepled fingers in the captain's chair. "It's possible that closer in, things do get more line of sight. And you're getting interference from the storm."

"Maybe," Tristan said. "But I also see ebbs and flows in the signal, depending on the location of the orbiting ship."

"Interesting," Dieter said.

"We have to at least be able to send a message to that ship, don't you think?" Lafayette said. "If it's anchoring this systemic field or whatever, sending a message to it should be the easiest thing to do."

"Maybe," Dieter said. He didn't even sound particularly skeptical about it. Just cheerily ready to get off the bridge. "Anybody who's up for some company, bring your dinner into my room. You can look at each other's notes, and we can discuss options before bedtime."

"That sounds lovely," Lafayette said.

But she wouldn't stay up too late talking. She already had plans for another long bath before bed.

CHAPTER 19

Tristan figured out the navigational workstation well enough for them to track the progress of the storm. It was swirling all around them. Looking at it on the screen was kind of remote, but nowhere near as remote as it felt being inside that spaceship.

Somewhere above her, up on the surface, brutal winds filled with ice and snow were buffeting absolutely everything. But down inside their warm ship encased in ice, it was like nothing was happening at all.

Lafayette made slower progress with the communications systems. She figured out how to isolate the messages and play them separately, but they still were unintelligible.

But after some work, she and Kora had them separated into two categories. There were messages that sounded like a spoken language, albeit ones that neither of them could understand.

And then there were others that still sounded like human voices, but what those voices were speaking didn't sound like words at all.

"There's no rhythm or pattern to the sounds," Kora said as Lafayette played one of the messages for Dieter and Tristan.

"It sounds like it deliberately doesn't have those things," Lafayette said. "Like someone is doing this on purpose."

"Like a code," Dieter said.

"What do you mean?" Tristan asked.

"Well, my family communicates with written images, but they don't correspond to any alphabet. It isn't even phonetic," he said.

"And you do that to keep Central Planning from knowing what you're communicating if they come across any of the writing," Lafayette said. "So you think these are secret messages too?"

"I would think so," Dieter said with a shrug. "Or something happened to the systemic field that we can't understand. Like shredding a page of writing and then trying to piece it back together again. But since none of us understands systemic fields, maybe we should stick to the first theory."

"I wish there had been books here," Kora said glumly from where she was sitting by Lafayette's feet.

"There's something else," Lafayette said as she reached down to give Kora's ears a scratch.

"What's that?" Dieter asked.

"The messed-up messages that don't sound like language? They all come from close by," she said.

"How close? Like on the ice floe?" Tristan asked, suddenly alarmed.

"I don't know exactly," Lafayette said. "But Kora and I are pretty sure they are coming from things inside the range established by the ship in orbit, this one, and the other two that appear on the map."

"So, someone on this planet is sending these messages?" Dieter said.

"I think so, yes."

"Then having them be secret totally makes sense," Dieter said.

"How does that make sense?" Tristan asked. "I mean, your family and other trading caravans send messages to each other, and they're perfectly intelligible."

"You'd think so, right?" Dieter said.

"Well, I mean, there's a cant with hidden meanings to the words, but they're still *words*," Tristan said.

"You're right," Dieter assured him. "But you're forgetting that caravans like my family's use line-of-sight communications. And that's exactly what we're not getting down here under all the ice."

"So these signals are coming from the other spaceships?" Lafayette asked. "But my father wouldn't try to send me a message I couldn't even understand. Not even the teaching construct up there with him, Frank Paine, would do that."

"We were inside the ship in the capital city," Tristan pointed out. "I know you said we were being watched, and I believe you. But no one was actually on that ship when we were there. And I kind of got the impression that you'd never seen anyone inside of it."

"I didn't spend huge amounts of time there, but you're right," Dieter said. "Every time I was inside, it was empty."

"So no one from Central Planning was in the bridge, sending signals," Tristan said.

"So that just leaves the ship at the bottom of the ocean?" Lafayette said. "You said we were getting a signal from it, because it's on the navigational map. But it was weak, you said."

"Right. Like it's inert. Like this ship was before Dieter threw all the switches," Tristan said.

"Although it could also be an effect of the water," Dieter put in. "I think it's deeper under the surface than we are here. That might be a factor."

"Okay, but still. Could these garbled messages be coming from there?" Tristan asked.

"How many of them are there?" Dieter asked Lafayette.

"They come in spurts," she said. She checked her notes in her journal and then touched the button to change one of the other displays on the console. "Look, they cluster every few hours."

"Like a call and response?" Dieter said musingly.

"If one source is sending and a bunch are replying, I can't tell," Lafayette said. "Maybe?"

"I think we have to assume these messages are from Central Planning," Dieter said, crossing his arms like he expected a fight.

But Lafayette wasn't sure what fight he was preparing for. "But we can't understand them," she said.

"No, they clearly don't want us to," he said.

"But if they never were on the ship that Lafayette and her father found, and they've never been here, what makes us think it's them? They're at the bottom of the ocean? Because we already covered that they didn't seem to be using the bridge of the ship in the capital city," Tristan said.

"No, why would they?" Dieter said. "They already took all they needed from that ship. I think we all know they aren't destroying things. I mean, they made a big show of burning all those books, sure. But that was only because they didn't *need* those books. They already know everything that was in them."

"You can't know that," Lafayette said.

"No, it's just a theory," Dieter said. "But it's a sound one. There's a reason they don't let more than a very selectively chosen few go up to the higher city."

"You think the signals are coming from the upper city?" Tristan asked. But not like he doubted it.

"Some of them, sure," Dieter said. "But if they've had centuries to work out how these consoles work, which I think they've had back in the capital city, they clearly know far more about them than we do after a mere day and a half poking around with them."

"I mean, we've all studied what little was known about these things from books before we got here," Tristan said half-defensively.

"If they know how they work, they likely know how to make more," Dieter said.

"Wait," Lafayette said. "You think these signals are coming from their airships?"

"It's a possibility," Dieter said.

"Wow," Tristan said, shaking his head. "It does make sense, though. If they're still out there, looking for us, they must've spread out over a wider area. Wider than line-of-sight communication. So they're using forbidden technology."

"I doubt they'd even have to wait until they were desperate to do that," Dieter said. "It's only forbidden for us to use this stuff. Not them. Never them."

"You think they know we turned this ship on," Lafayette said. She felt a chill run up her spine.

"I think it's a strong possibility," Dieter said.

And here Lafayette had thought that all of his sitting in the captain's chair had just been him waiting for a Dieter-sized job to perform. But he'd been working all this out the whole time.

"But that means—" Tristan started to say, then stopped, giving Lafayette a nervous look before turning away, suddenly finding something in his own notebook terribly interesting.

"That means what?" Lafayette asked. But she didn't have to wait for an answer. The minute the question was out of her mouth, she already knew what it was. "It means I can't go through with my plan to contact my dad." She bit down hard on her lip, but then she had to let it go. She wasn't done talking yet. "That's the whole reason we're here in the first place."

"I know," Dieter said. As much as she knew now why he was standing with his arms crossed, his voice was surprisingly gentle.

"I *have* to let him know I'm still looking for a way to get to him," she said. There was a coppery taste in her mouth now. She had bitten down too hard before. But she brushed away the drop of blood with an angry slash of the back of her hand and glared up at Dieter.

"We'll find a way to do that," Dieter said. "If they can send secret messages, we'll find out a way to do the same. But in the meantime, we have to assume that if we send anything at all, they're going to know it's coming from us."

"If they already have navigational systems, they already knew exactly where this ship was," Tristan said.

"It might've not appeared on their maps when it was dormant," Dieter said.

"But it does now," Tristan said.

Dieter just shrugged.

"They know we're here," Lafayette said, hugging herself as if the bridge had suddenly grown cold again. "It's only the storm that's holding them back. When it breaks, they'll be here."

"Yes," Dieter said.

"And there's nowhere we can go to escape them," Lafayette said.

"The airship is almost certainly wrecked," he agreed.

"I'm sorry," Lafayette said. "I thought this would work out differently. Now you've lost so much, and I gained nothing in exchange."

"Well, not nothing," Dieter said.

"I guess we've learned some things," Tristan said. But he didn't sound like even he, who valued learning things over anything else, truly believed that was enough.

"The storm is still going strong," Lafayette said. "We have some time to figure out what to do next. I guess we can turn on all the replicators and stockpile food. Maybe find a way to make some sort of conveyance. Although how we're going to get off the ice, I don't know."

"We have time," Dieter agreed. "We also have ways to watch for their approach." He gestured to the navigational console, still showing the dots of the spaceships.

"But we can't even see the airships on that," Lafayette said.

"We're watching the storm," Tristan said, clicking over to the other display. "This storm is huge. It covers the whole ice floe. But when it breaks up, this map is going to be showing us clear skies over the ice floe."

"And the airships traveling through those clear skies," Dieter said. "We'll have a day's warning of their approach. At least."

"Okay," Lafayette said. "But what do we do with that?"

"First, we watch," Dieter said. "I want to be absolutely sure they already know where we are before we do anything. There's always a chance I'm wrong and they don't know where this ship is. Then we can sit still and watch them spiral around in search patterns, just like we did."

"But if you're not wrong?" Lafayette said. "If they come straight for us?"

Dieter gave her a sad sort of smile, then pointed with his chin towards her workstation.

"Then, we send that message to your father. Because there'll be no reason not to."

"We'll still be in custody again," Lafayette said.

"Maybe," Dieter said. "Maybe not. But either way, I have no intention of stopping until we achieve the goal of getting you to your father. I assumed you felt the same way."

"I sure do," Tristan said. "I just hope this storm rages for a few more days. I'm curious what the next console over does."

Lafayette glanced from her communications workstation to the one beside it. She thought it might have something to do with what happened back in the engineering room. But a few more days to find out for sure *would* be nice.

"I still think, with enough time, I could figure out how to fly this thing," Lafayette said.

"I think I could too," Dieter said, slumping back down into the captain's chair and fiddling with the back support controls. "If only we weren't thoroughly encased in ice."

CHAPTER 20

t took nearly six days for the storm to finally break. Dieter, who had taken to dozing in the captain's chair for half the night, shouted loudly enough for Tristan and Lafayette to both hear him. The two of them met in the corridor, then raced together to the bridge.

"I thought it would taper out more slowly than it did," Dieter said as they gathered around him at the workstation that stood just to the left of the navigational systems. This one could display images of areas within the fleet's systemic field.

Although none of them, not even Kora, had any real clue how it did that.

And, until this moment, they had no idea what kind of clarity those images would show. Because, from the moment Tristan had worked out how to make it display anything, there had been nothing to see but blowing snow and ice. It cycled through a set number of images every few seconds meant to show them the world around their ship from a slightly different angle. But every switch was only a slight variation on the blowing snow theme.

Now, though. Now they were looking at the windswept expanse of the ice floe under startlingly blue skies. There wasn't a cloud in sight.

But they all quickly focused on the same part of the rotating images: the remains of Dieter's family's airship. It spread across several of the images in the rotation, silvery bits of metallic fabric blown into tatters that clung to bits of ice. Even the gondola itself was broken up, albeit into larger pieces.

"Well, that's it, then," Dieter said. "No salvaging that. We're stuck here."

"Diet, I'm so sorry," Tristan said, putting a hand on his friend's arm.

"Don't worry about it," Dieter said. "I've had the entire lifetime of this storm to prepare for this moment. I knew it was inevitable."

"What about Central Planning?" Lafayette asked. "Are they on their way yet?"

"Oh, yes," Dieter said, redirecting their attention to the navigational system. "They split up into four squads to wait out at the edges of the storm, but they're all closing in now. We have a little less than a day before they're on top of us."

"What can we do with less than a day?" Tristan wondered.

Lafayette knew they had all been avoiding that question. Well, she and Tristan had, anyway. Tristan had worked out the cameras and gotten far more adept at the navigational systems in that time. That had called for a lot of focused study. And for her part, she had learned a bit more about the communications systems.

But once she had figured out that the workstation two consoles over was a sort of computerized library, she had spent all her time there with Kora curled up at her feet. It was a library of general knowledge, not anything really useful like engineering manuals or science textbooks or the ship's logs, which Dieter hadn't found yet either. Still, she had spent her days filling journal after journal with the answers to every random question that had occurred to her and Kora.

Maybe too random. But she had known she would never have enough time with the console for a systematic approach to learning all it contained. So she had taken a more scattershot, ask it anything approach. Now her head was spinning from all the facts she had stuffed into it about the life cycle of stars, the intricacies of cell structure in living things, the mechanics of lighter-than-air flight.

She had assumed the last would come in handy. But if they ended up moving from ice floe to some sort of water transportation, that would be as useless as the rest of what she had just learned.

Still, while she and Tristan had been pressing buttons and writing in their journals, Dieter had mostly been sitting in that captain's chair, either dozing or in deep thought. If anyone had come up with a plan for what they should do now, it was Dieter.

"I'm going to go back to the surface to cover up the hole down to the airlock as best as I can," he said. "I was planning to drag the debris down to the cavern if possible. Ironically, I was mostly worried the pieces would be too big to fit through the fissure. It seems I have the opposite problem now."

"If we all work together—" Lafayette started to say.

"It would still take too much time," Dieter cut her off. "Look at those fragments of the balloon. There are millions of them. We'd never get them all."

"I don't think it's going to matter too much," Tristan said. "The airship debris field extends over half the ice directly over this starship. And they already know where we are, right? So hiding the airship doesn't hide the fact that we're here, or even where specifically we are."

"I agree," Dieter said. "I just don't want to make it any easier than it has to be, getting in to us."

"That console that was for security," Lafayette said, looking around as she tried to remember just which one it was. "We can seal all the airlocks. Even with pry bars, they won't be able to get in. We could only do it because the survivors of this ship basically left it unlocked when they abandoned it. Sealed up, we'll be impenetrable."

"I know," Dieter said. "But buying us a little more time is worth the effort."

"You just want to frustrate anyone in Central Planning," Tristan said. "And with the image display here, you'll be able to watch them get frustrated."

"You're not wrong," Dieter said with a shrug and a half-hearted attempt at a grin. "I'm going to suit up and get going. I don't imagine it will take me long."

He shuffled off to his room in the officers' quarters to fetch his cold-weather gear. Tristan was looking at the images cycling over the field of airship wreckage, but Lafayette didn't think he was really seeing it. His mind was elsewhere.

"We can tell from the navigation maps that the Central Planning ships are closing in on us, right?" Lafayette said.

"Hm?" Tristan said, then shifted his attention to the other console. "Yeah, they definitely are all heading directly here. Did you want to try sending that signal to the other ship now?"

"Not yet," Lafayette said. Although she and Kora had already recorded the message she planned to send. All she had to do was press a button, and somewhere up in orbit, the communications console on the bridge of that other starship would receive it. But so would Central Planning.

"You said you encrypted it," Tristan pointed out. "So it should be safe."

Which was true as far as it went. Lafayette and Kora had used the library console to bone up on encryption as a concept, then used that knowledge to poke harder at the garbled messages they knew were coming from Central Planning.

Then she had realized that the communications console was designed to decrypt these same messages. And once she knew how to do that, they could hear everything that the Central Planning airships were messaging to each other. Which—not surprisingly given the persistent, strong storm—had all been about the weather and the time frame for their mission given their dwindling supplies.

Working her way through the encryption programs on the communications console, she saw that Central Planning was using the most basic version that all the starships had on their consoles. There were other, more elaborate versions, ones that would take even the other starships minutes to decrypt. And she had guessed that while it was technically possible for anyone in Central Planning to decrypt a message in the more complicated code, maybe they didn't have what they needed to do that on the airships. Maybe they'd have to have someone in the capital city decrypt it for them.

That was all a guess. And even if she was right, it only would buy them a few minutes, maybe an hour.

And, if her father didn't have access to the bridge on his starship yet, it would all be academic, anyway.

Still, she hadn't figured out a path with a better chance of success than sending her father a message with the tightest encryption that she still knew he could decrypt, at least potentially. With the help of the Frank Paine teaching construct, it was just possible.

But nothing she said would stay secret long.

"I still want to wait," she said to Tristan. "I'll push that button as we're leaving the ship. It's the best plan."

"Your father is safer than we are just now," he said. "They can't get to him."

"They can't get to us either," Lafayette said. "Once we seal the airlocks, there's no way they're getting in here."

Tristan looked like he wanted to say something about that, but changed his mind with a shake of his head.

"We'll have to wait and see, I guess," he said at last.

Still, they packed up their things in case they *did* have to make a run for it. Lafayette, days before, had figured out how to ask the food replicators for specific things, and they all had bags filled to bursting with the most nutrient-dense, high-calorie protein bars, enough to keep them fed for weeks if need be. That, plus her bag of journals and her bedroll, made for almost more than Lafayette could carry.

She really hoped they didn't have to escape over the ice floe. That would be a miserable journey in so very many ways. But if they had to, they were prepared.

Lafayette set her bags beside the communications console, the outermost layers of her cold-weather gear folded neatly on top of them. She was dressed almost too warmly already, but once she stopped moving around, hauling heavy things from her room to the bridge, she would cool back down again.

"Status report?" Dieter called as he strode onto the bridge with his parka, scarf and hat draped over one arm.

"They're definitely closing in," Tristan said. "And they're making better time than we figured. They're going to be here inside of ten hours."

"There's no wind," Dieter said. "Dead calm air again. This place is downright weird. Or we caught it at a weird moment."

He threw his cold-weather gear onto the captain's chair, then saw their packed bags. Without a word, he headed back to his room to gather his own things together.

The storm had died out in the predawn hours of the morning, so it was far past sunset when the ten hours were up and the airships arrived at their location. They had already eaten dinner, everyone taking double servings of everything just in case something interfered with breakfast in the morning. The load of food had left Lafayette feeling soporific, dozing in her chair at the communications console. But Tristan sitting up when he saw the first ship land, soft a sound as it was, had her awake in a snap.

"Nice formation," Dieter said grudgingly as the first of the four squads landed, three ships in a V coming down at an even pace to land simultaneously on the ice. "Where do you suppose they train on these ships? No one I know has ever seen it happen. And I know people from all over."

"Maybe that island prison, if it's not just a rumor," Lafayette said.

"Or maybe, if it's not just a rumor, there are more hidden places like that. Places so well hidden there aren't even rumors about them," Tristan said.

They watched as the second squad set down beside the first, their three ships flying together in an equally tight formation.

"What's that?" Lafayette asked, drawing their attention to the navigational console. They could see the dots for the six ships on the ground as well as the six ships preparing to set down beside them in turn. But there was also another, thirteenth dot. It was coming in from the south and west, not quite on the ice floe yet but moving at incredible speed.

"That trajectory comes from the capital city," Dieter said. "Wow, that ship is making amazing time."

None of them even had a guess. But on the other display, they could see people in bulky parkas with hoods drawn tight around their masked and goggled faces emerging from the gondolas of the airships. Most set to work securing the mooring lines. But others fanned out, examining the debris field and poking around in the remains of the wrecked gondola from Dieter's family's ship.

"Looking for our bodies?" Tristan speculated.

But Dieter was already shaking his head. "No. They know we're down here. And we know they're on a tight timetable. Unlike us, they don't have access to endless food sources."

"So what *are* they going to do?" Lafayette asked.

"I have a different question," Dieter said, pointing at the thirteenth ship on the navigational map. It was over the ice floe now, zipping towards them along the most direct path. "Why isn't this ship signaling anyone they're on their way? Do the other Central Planning ships even know it's coming?"

Lafayette turned to her communications console, but all the messages between the ships were the same as before. All with only the most basic level of encryption, all focused on coordinating the mooring of the ships and mustering the crews together.

"They're meeting on the ice," Lafayette said. "But no one is saying what they'll be doing then."

"It's almost like they know we can hear them," Dieter said.

"So, that ship flying in isn't communicating on purpose?" Lafayette said.

Dieter just shrugged. "I mean, I think it would be too much to hope for that they're not Central Planning at all. That we're about to be rescued by some hero of the people."

"Because nothing your family has can travel that fast," Lafayette guessed.

"Only Central Planning has ships like that," Dieter agreed.

Lafayette watched the dot making its steady progress across the map and wished she knew what it all meant.

CHAPTER 21

They spent the next few hours watching the bulky forms of people moving around the ice floe and idly arguing about what they might be doing.

It kind of looked like searching. They were traveling in packs of three or four in what looked like a search grid. And they were digging through larger bits of airship debris when they came across it. Maybe they really were searching for bodies.

But at least four of those groups passed right over the fissure that led down to the ice cavern. And none of them seemed to notice it.

"I plugged it with ice chunks, sure," Dieter told Lafayette and Tristan. "But there's no way I could make it invisible. Not when I was doing it from the other side. I couldn't see the surface or get at it at all. They must be seeing it but ignoring it."

Which was maddening. But the long hours of the moonlit night ticked away until finally, when the eastern sky was just turning a softer shade of indigo but the sun was still an hour or more away, the thirteenth ship finally came into view on the image display.

It was another airship, but of a vastly different design. The gondola was about the size of the one on Dieter's family's airship, so about a quarter of the size of the other Central Planning airships already moored on the ice. But the balloon itself was… well, less balloon-y.

"There's a structure inside that thing," Dieter said, leaning in to squint at the image. "Some kind of rigid framework is defining the shape, not just the air inside the balloon itself."

"It might not all be one balloon," Tristan theorized. "There could be a bunch of air cells inside that structure. Like a redundancy against damage. That's probably a lot safer in this environment than…"

He didn't finish his thought, but he didn't need to. They were all looking at the debris field that was the remains of their own airship.

"It must be new?" Lafayette said. It looked shiny in the moonlight, but then all the airships did.

The thirteenth airship circled the other twelve moored on the ice as if assessing the situation before finally setting down outside of the perimeter defined by the other ships. It fired harpoons and lines to make itself fast, then winched down until the gondola was touching the surface of the ice.

Then, a single figure emerged. Like everyone else, this figure was wrapped in the thickest of parkas and heavy, form-obscuring pants over boots. Their hood was up and drawn close around their face-covering layers of scarf and tinted goggles. There was absolutely nothing identifiable about them in any way.

So when Lafayette sucked in a breath of recognition, both Tristan and Dieter shot her confused looks.

"It's Margo," she explained. "Margo Weiss. I'm sure of it."

"I don't know," Dieter said skeptically.

"They're certainly shorter than anyone else out there," Tristan allowed. But then he shook his head. "That doesn't make any sense though. Why would she be here?"

"She works for Central Planning now," Lafayette pointed out. Not adding that she had gotten that job by selling out all three of them as well as Tristan's mentor Uche Okafo. That she was the reason all of Lafayette's parents' journals and Uche's stash of books had been burned in the street.

That she had intended to separate Lafayette and Kora so that Kora could be studied. And that study would've ended in the dissection of Kora's dead body.

"No, there's no reason for her to be here," Dieter said. "She betrayed us, I know that. I promise I don't hate her any less than you," he rushed to add, and Lafayette realized she had fisted her hands and shifted to an aggressive posture. She forced herself to relax and hear him out.

"She works for Central Planning," she said again, as calmly as she could.

"But her job was in the city," Tristan said. "She wanted access to the upper city, and betraying us is what got that for her. So why would she be here? This isn't what she wanted."

"We got away," Lafayette said. "Did that change the terms of her employment?"

"Ah," Dieter said. Then a grin spread across his face. "Oh, I like that idea a lot."

"I mean," Tristan said, gesturing at the images of the moored airships. "If she's here to get us back, it really looks like they're about to do it. So maybe belay the celebration on that score."

"I don't know," Dieter said, still grinning. "Anything I can do to make her life difficult, I'm all for."

"Anyway, we still don't know that it's her," Tristan said. "It could be a different woman, or a short man. We don't know."

"Whoever it is, they walk just like her," Lafayette insisted.

"Seriously?" Dieter said. Just the one word, but she knew what he meant. The figure they were watching was having the same struggles walking in heavy boots over the uneven ice with its hidden crevices and toe-catching ridges as anyone else. And just wearing such thick layers of pants forced anyone's gait a little wider than usual. Lafayette knew all that.

And yet, there was something in the roll of the hips. Something in the way the hooded head kept tipping to one side and then shaking back like the person inside all those clothes wanted to toss a bit of hair out of their eyes more out of long habit than any current necessity.

"It's her," Lafayette said, crossing her arms as if that could somehow signal the end of the argument.

As they watched the lone figure approach the other ships, two more figures emerged from two of the moored airships. They met together first, briefly conferring, before turning to wait for the figure from the thirteenth ship to approach them.

Then there was a very long conversation that involved only a few sparing but maddeningly vague hand gestures. Sometimes they pointed up. Sometimes they pointed down. They could be discussing the starship in orbit and the starship in the ice. Or they could be arguing about the likelihood of the weather holding and of the ice floe not breaking up.

The sun dawned in the east with a sudden red ferocity, shooting beams of light directly at the threesome on the ice. The taller two lifted mittened hands to block out the light, but the third seemed unbothered. But now, one of the taller two pointed at the airship they had emerged from, and the other tall one nodded enthusiastically.

The one that Lafayette was still sure was Margo Weiss gave in with a show of good grace, and the three figures trekked to the nearest airship, disappearing inside.

"Now we can't see or hear," Tristan complained.

But Dieter gestured for Lafayette to turn back to the communications console. She turned up the gain, and they all listened to the silence for what felt like forever. Then they heard a man's voice speaking staccato nonsense, loud and clear but completely unintelligible.

Until Lafayette pressed the button to decrypt the signal. Then they heard the same voice again, saying, "Fleet Commander Stowe to Central Command, please respond."

The three of them silently celebrated this little victory, but quickly stopped when a woman's voice responded.

Lafayette waited for her to stop speaking, then hit the decryption button. "Fleet Commander Stowe, this is Central Command. You may proceed."

The man spoke again, and when he stopped, Lafayette hit the button. "Central Command, I am here with Captain Tavers as well as your operative..."

He trailed off here, and there was another voice in the background, a woman's voice but speaking too softly to be discernible even after decryption.

Then Fleet Commander Stowe was back. "She says she's Acting Special Missions Officer Weiss. I do hope that's meaningful to you."

Lafayette shot a look to Dieter and Tristan, who just nodded acknowledgement that she had been right. They all listened for what was coming next.

Central Command took a long moment to respond to that message. And when she did speak again, it was only to say, "Understood, Fleet Commander. You may proceed."

They waited for the next message. Lafayette tried to imagine the scene on that airship, the fleet commander and the airship captain conferring with Margo. What was she telling them? It was difficult to tell from such a brief message, but Lafayette had the strong feeling that this Fleet Commander Stowe wasn't exactly happy at Margo's arrival.

Margo, who had bragged about jumping two ranks when she'd earned her position in Central Planning by betraying them all. That kind of thing probably rubbed other people the wrong way, and not just the ones that suddenly found themselves outranked by a newbie.

Then Stowe's encrypted voice burst out at them once more. Lafayette waited for him to stop speaking and then pressed the decryption button.

"Central Command, we have general orders to seek out and secure all evidence of ancient technology, and to destroy such evidence if it cannot be secured. Further, we have specific orders to be on the lookout for a certain rogue airship that may lead us to one such unsecured site."

Lafayette and Tristan exchanged a look, each silently mouthing the word "destroy," but Dieter just stared fixedly at the console, as if he could will it to deliver what they needed to hear faster.

"Fleet Commander Stowe, acknowledged. Those are your orders," Central Command said. A bit unhelpfully, Lafayette couldn't help thinking. Not that she was siding with Stowe here. But she couldn't suppress a twinge of sympathy at his frustration.

They knew the speaker had changed even before the console ran its decryption, Stowe stepping aside to allow Margo Weiss to address Central Command.

"Central Command, this is Acting Special Missions Officer Margo Weiss. Please confirm my authority to direct activities here."

"Great," Tristan grumbled as they waited for the response.

"ASMO Weiss, your authority is confirmed, but we remind you that your purview is severely restricted. The fleet's general and specific orders are still in effect. Unless you have something further to report?"

"Well, she certainly sounded testy that time, didn't she?" Dieter said in a low voice.

Then Margo was back. "Understood, Central Command. I am not trying to forestall the fleet's orders. I only ask for a brief reprieve. I don't even need them to slow down the work of placing the explosives. I only ask to delay the order of detonation should it be necessary. Which it might not be! I think I'll have everything well in hand before they're even ready to go."

"Fleet Commander Stowe, what is the expected time of mission completion?" Central Command asked.

Then Stowe was back on the line. "Central Command, we need twelve hours to place those explosives and get the fleet to minimum safe distance."

The response came almost instantly this time. "Acting Special Missions Officer Weiss, you have until that time to meet your own objective. No extensions are possible. The general and specific orders take precedence."

As informally chatty as her last message had been, Margo got even more so with her next one. "But you have to give me enough time! My friends are on that ship. I'm quite sure by now they've sealed themselves inside. I need just a little time to talk them out of it."

The three of them exchanged nervous glances as they waited to hear what Central Command would say next.

Then the voice from the capital city came back on. "You have until the Fleet Commander has ensured the safety of all airships and counted down to detonation, no more. We are aware of the targets you are pursuing, and their value to us is nothing compared to the need to secure this site at once."

Margo's voice burst back, almost a wail. "But no one knows they're here! There's no need to rush this destruction! I can get them out, and we can run a full investigation of this site. Who's going to come all the way out here and find this thing in the meantime? Fleet Commander Stowe already has the area secured. There's no risk here."

Lafayette was sure that saying that man's name out loud had been a desperate bid for flattery to gain her something. But it didn't work. When Central Command came back on the line, it was only to reiterate, "Fleet Commander Stowe has command of the site and of the timeframe for the execution of his orders. Work around it or do not. You are reminded that your situation is highly precarious, *Acting* Special Missions Officer Weiss, and your performance is under continuous, active review. Conduct yourself accordingly. Central Command out."

That sounded pretty final. Even so, the three of them said nothing for several long minutes before deciding that really was the end of the conversation.

"We're her friends now?" Tristan said disdainfully.

"I mean, it sounds like she's here to make sure we don't blow up," Lafayette said, perhaps too optimistically to judge by the sneer Dieter threw her way.

"She's here because the deal she made to join Central Planning was contingent on us as well as Uche being in custody. She *needs* us," he said.

"We don't need her," Tristan said, his voice only slightly tinged by the hurt Lafayette knew he must be feeling. Out of the three of them, he was the one who had come close to actually being a friend of Margo's. Back before her betrayal.

"Exactly," Dieter said.

But Tristan wasn't done. As miserable as he still sounded, he lifted his chin and pinned first Lafayette and then Dieter with a steady gaze before finishing his thought.

"We don't need her. But maybe we can use her."

CHAPTER 22

Dieter and Tristan started bouncing ideas off each other at once, listing what their options were and weighing those options and rejecting the wildest, if perhaps not as quickly as Lafayette would've.

But she stepped back from all that. She couldn't focus on it, not yet. Instead, she watched on the image displays, waiting for the moment when Margo emerged from the fleet commander's airship. An airship that was no bigger than any of the others. None of its markings were different in any way. As unusual as the ship was that Margo had arrived on, the other twelve were completely interchangeable with each other.

Finally, the door of the gondola swung open, and a small, parka-clad figure emerged. She made a few shuffling steps forward, then made a motion that Lafayette recognized at once with a flinch of sympathy. One of Margo's boots had caught on a jut of ice while the other had started sliding on the slick surface the instant her distribution of weight had changed. She froze in place, arms out for balance until the risk of falling on her butt was gone.

Then she straightened and resumed shuffling, back in the direction of her own airship.

"If she wants to help us, we should just go talk to her," Lafayette said.

"Not going to happen," Dieter said at once.

"Why not? I can see the crews from the other airships. They're right over top of us, shooting some kind of straight-down cannons into the ice," Lafayette said.

"Placing the explosives, surely," Tristan put in.

"But Margo's ship is way over there," Lafayette went on. "She's well away from the other ships. And the opening of the fissure out of the ice cavern is just outside that perimeter. We could get from there to her ship, probably without anyone even noticing us since they stopped making those search sweeps."

"The fissure I blocked with ice, you mean?" Dieter said.

"What good would talking with Margo do?" Tristan said, but earnestly. Like he really wanted to hear an answer that would sway him. Or was hoping for one, although less likely, to sway Dieter.

"How good are their explosives?" Lafayette asked, gesturing at the image of the crews working the cannons. "*Can* they destroy this ship?"

"It would be handy if they just blasted the ice off of us," Dieter said with half a grin. "Once we're free, we could try flying this thing. Maybe, they're doing us a favor."

Tristan made a gesture just short of an eye roll as he huffed out a breath. "Do you realize this hull is far more sensitive to damage than even the balloon on your airship? If we are in the vacuum of space with a hole anywhere on this ship, it's going to be pretty catastrophic. And how are we going to make sure we don't have holes? This ship is way bigger than your balloon."

"Fine, have it your way," Dieter said.

"I wasn't joking," Lafayette said.

"I wasn't joking either," Dieter countered. But his persistent grin undercut that message more than a little bit.

"Do we think they can actually destroy this ship?" Lafayette asked levelly.

Tristan made a humming noise, one she had come to associate with him puzzling something through.

But Dieter was the one who spoke first. "I think they're intending only to break the ice. With the ice broken, the weight of this ship will be enough to sink it with nothing further needed from them."

"That's not destroyed," Lafayette pointed out.

"No, but it *is* secured. No one is going to find it then," Dieter said.

"I think Dieter has a point," Tristan said. "I don't think Central Planning knew where that ship was that your father found, or they would've done something about it. Remember, he was trying to follow a trail of where our ancestors had gone after leaving that ship behind. And it took his whole lifetime, because anything anyone knew about at all, Central Planning had already removed all evidence of it. He had only rumors and vague whispers of clues to follow."

"So you think they never found the ship because if they had, they would've destroyed it somehow?" Lafayette asked.

"No," Dieter said. "Think of the ship in the capital city. They had access to that. They stripped it of everything, sure. But they didn't destroy it. I don't think they ever even tried to. They just... well, secured it."

"Hid it in plain sight," Tristan said.

"Because they still wanted it, or because they knew they couldn't just get rid of it?" Lafayette asked.

But none of them knew the answer to that question.

"I think this is just going to blow the ice away from the hull," Dieter said again after they'd all spent several moments just pondering.

"Okay," Lafayette said tiredly. "Are you willing to bet our lives on being right about that?"

"We could probably still live here," Tristan said. "We'd be on the bottom of the ocean for... well, quite some time if not forever. But we'll have air and warmth and plenty of food."

"I don't want to be trapped on the bottom of the ocean forever," Lafayette said.

"There's no talking to Margo," Dieter said. "There's only turning ourselves in to Margo. Which means we'll be right back where we were, handcuffed in the backs of vans heading to uncertain fates. Or, in Kora's case, a pretty unavoidably certain fate."

"I'm not afraid," Kora announced. But none of them quite believed her.

"You wanted to use her," Lafayette said to Tristan. He knew she meant Margo.

"Yeah, but I don't know *how*," Tristan said. He shot a glare at Dieter, and Lafayette kind of wished she had listened a little more closely to what they'd been saying to each other before. Although maybe it didn't matter, since the result of all their arguing had been no working plan.

"We can take her airship," Dieter said, completely out of nowhere.

"Oh, just like that?" Tristan scoffed.

"We can *trick* her out of her airship," Dieter said, as if that clarified anything. "Look at the size of it."

"It's pretty much the same as the one we flew here on," Tristan said.

"Exactly," Dieter said. "So is she alone, or does she have a crew with her? If she does, it can be more than two people, three at the absolute max?"

"How cranky would three people be after being trapped with Margo on the flight here from the capital city?" Lafayette wondered. "I mean, they were going pretty fast when they arrived. But still. Such a tiny space, for four days?"

"I'd want to kill her," Dieter said merrily.

"They are still Central Planning," Tristan pointed out. "Not an organization that's known for mutiny. At all."

"He's right," Dieter said with a sigh. "They have a strong sense of…" He made a rolling gesture with his hand, like he was trying to summon up the perfect word.

"Loyalty?" Lafayette offered.

"I was going to say mental conformity," Tristan said.

"Exactly," Dieter said, pointing at Tristan. "You're right. They aren't breakable. We won't be able to get them on our side, no matter how annoyed they are at *Acting* Special Missions Officer Weiss." He mimicked the Central Command woman's disdainful tone almost exactly.

"So what *are* you thinking?" Lafayette asked him.

"We can take them," Dieter said, planting a fist into his opposite hand's open palm. "With Kora, we outnumber them."

"Three crew members plus Margo?" Tristan said with a frown.

"We don't know it's three. It could be two. Or even one," Dieter said.

"One pilot with no relief?" Lafayette said skeptically.

"Fine, two pilots on rotation," Dieter said. "We outnumber them."

"It's more likely to be three, though," Tristan said. "We had three of us on rotation, and I think you'd have to agree that two—"

"Fine! With Kora, our numbers are even," Dieter said grudgingly. "Still, we're rested up and very well fed. Can they say the same?"

Lafayette and Tristan traded a glance, each thinking of just how exhausted and hungry they had been when they had finally reached the ice floe. Not even after being on half rations and spending their days swinging picks at ice, but before that. Just rotating duties in the airship cockpit and subsisting on full rations.

"We might have a chance," Lafayette conceded at last.

"Our best chance is if we go now," Tristan said, but with a sigh that said he hated his own words even as they came out of his mouth. "They'll have time to rest up during the day today since apparently they aren't part of the explosives-placing teams."

"They're probably all three napping right now," Dieter said.

"Then we should go," Tristan said. But he made no move for his parka. He just looked around the bridge as if afraid this was his last glimpse of something as important to him as his longtime childhood home. "Should we?"

"I like it here," Lafayette said. "I could study these consoles every day, eating anything I want, basking in warm baths. I could do that for a long, long time."

"But not forever," Tristan finished for her.

"Not forever," she agreed.

"Fine," he said. And, as one, they all started gearing up in heavy pants and boots, scarves and hats and parkas.

But before taking up her packs or even putting on her gloves, Lafayette went to the communications console one last time. The other two paused in what they were doing to watch as she keyed up the message she had recorded for her father. She double-checked the encryption and all the delivery details.

Then she pushed the button to send it on its way.

"That's it," she said. "Now they know for sure we're in here."

"They already knew," Dieter said.

"But now your father knows we're finding a way to get to him," Tristan said. "A message sent from ship to ship? He knows we're getting close."

"If he gets it," Lafayette said, but so quietly she wasn't sure if the other two even heard her. Which was just as well. She always beamed her optimism at both of them at her highest possible settings. But her worries? Her pessimism? Those were better kept close to her chest.

The three of them plus Kora trekked up all the ladders in the engineering section, then past the brig to the spoke corridor until they reached the domestic quarters in the wheel.

It was warmer this time, following the ropes back down to the airlock. And light was always preferable to darkness in Lafayette's view. But, being trapped in ice, there hadn't been anything they could do about the gravity. They had to climb along the steep cliff meant to be the walkable floor of a corridor, but that was okay.

She wasn't in anywhere near the hurry she had been the last time, when everything had been on the edge of exploding.

At the bottom of the rope climb, Lafayette took a moment to adjust all of her packs on her back while Dieter fought to get the door back open. It came free with a metallic shriek, and all three of them were greeted with a lungful of bitterly cold air.

"Didn't miss this," Tristan said, but didn't hesitate to follow Dieter into the tunnel through the ice.

It was awkward, and impossible to do with the packs on, so all that adjustment Lafayette had done after her climb was pointless. She had to set them all together on the ground in front of her, place the top of her head against them, and push them ahead of her as she crawled on her hands and knees. It was almost too narrow for even this maneuver to work once she was past the bubble outside the airlock door.

But then she was inside the ice cavern, once more lit up in eerie green color from Kora's maximized indicator light. They each dug their lanterns out of their gear, then carried their bags to the bottom of the spiraling ice tunnel to the surface.

"How much did you block this?" Tristan asked.

"I'll go first," Dieter said, not quite answering the question. Although he had an ice axe already in his hand, one with a shorter handle so he could swing it in tight spaces.

"We're going to overshoot their nap time, aren't we?" Lafayette said.

It was harder going up the spiral than it had been sliding down, although being larger than the tunnel to the airlock at least there was room to see around her bags. She kept them in front of her because she was paranoid about one of them sliding all the way back to the bottom, and it was almost too dark to see anyway, but it still felt less claustrophobic. Especially when Tristan, who was in front of her, would throw a look back at her now and again, just checking in that she was still doing okay.

Then they stopped, and Lafayette heard the sounds of Dieter swinging that axe. Tristan pushed pieces of ice back towards her, and she pushed them far enough behind her for them to slide all the way back down to the cavern below.

But this didn't take as long as she had feared. The ringing of the axe fell away, and there was sunlight shining on her face, if only diffusely.

Then Tristan and Dieter both were helping pull her bags out of the hole, and she was climbing up after, and they were all back on the surface under a cloudless blue sky.

But they were also crouching low, all too aware of the bright colors of their parkas. The Central Planning parkas were little better. Being all black, they were easy to spot against the ice, especially by daylight.

No one was near them at the moment. Clusters of crew members were working the cannons, but they were too distant for their voices to be heard.

"Margo," Lafayette said the minute her eyes landed on one parka'd figure smaller than the others. She was also closer to the three of them, but she was standing with her back to their position.

Something about the slope of her shoulders under that parka just struck Lafayette as profoundly sad. But she elected not to speak that thought out loud. She could already imagine what Dieter would say if she did.

"Come on," Dieter said, grabbing his own packs and then making his way, still crouched low, to the gondola of Margo's airship.

It took less than a minute to reach the door, which opened at once to Dieter's touch. Then they were all inside. Dieter lunged to the cockpit, while Tristan and Lafayette went to the back of the gondola. Kora dove into the tiny room between, although in this case it was a galley and not a toilet space.

Empty. It was totally empty.

"Well," Dieter said, and Lafayette realized he had been holding his ice axe in his hand the entire time. She felt queasy at the thought of what he had been intending to do with it. Or, at least, had been prepared to do with it.

"Don't you think that was a little—" Tristan started to say.

Then the door of the gondola banged open, and they all realized, far too late, that they had effectively trapped themselves inside.

CHAPTER 23

Strong hands closed down on Lafayette and dragged her outside, back into the ice and cold, but this time without her bags. Those hands were still on her arms like vises, so it was definitely a different person who grabbed the front of her hat and yanked it down hard over her eyes, effectively blinding her since she couldn't get even an elbow free to push it back again.

They kept dragging her further from the gondola. She heard the clatter of Dieter's axe falling to the floor, although the scuffling sounds of a fight both preceded and continued after he had been disarmed.

Tristan yelped, but whether in pain or surprise, Lafayette wasn't sure.

Then the hands on her shoulders pushed her down onto her knees on the ice floe. A jutting protrusion of ice stabbed right under her kneecap, but she ignored the rush of pain.

She didn't have her bags. She didn't have her journals. She thought they were still inside the gondola, just inside the door where she had dropped them, but she couldn't push her hat back to see for sure.

She heard a grunt she recognized as Dieter's as he landed on his knees just to her left. Then Tristan was there on her right side.

But where was Kora?

Footsteps crunched up to them over the snow and ice in a steady, unhurried pace. Then she heard Margo say, "You can let them go. They aren't going anywhere."

The hands on her arms released her, and Lafayette immediately reached up to push her hat back and get her goggles back in place over her eyes. Only then did she look up at Margo, who was towering over her.

Lafayette couldn't see Margo's face, though. The eyes were lost behind the glare of sun off her goggles, and while Margo wasn't wearing a wrapping of scarf like Lafayette was, she had on a different sort of garment that fit around her neck up to the bottoms of her ears and covered her nose and mouth entirely.

"Okay?" Tristan asked, and she looked over at him. Someone had struck him over his eye. He wasn't bleeding, but there was already a dark bruise forming there.

"I'm fine," Lafayette said.

She really wanted to ask him if he knew where Kora was. But she didn't dare say anything out loud about that.

"I'm fine too, if anyone cares," Dieter said, a touch too loudly. Like he was trying to draw attention to himself. Or away from something else.

Margo angled her body so that she was more directly facing Dieter. "My condolences for the loss of your ship. I know it won't be easy for your family to replace. But then again, since they were largely using it to perform illegal operations, maybe that's for the best."

Dieter sneered but said nothing.

Again, Lafayette heard the sound of approaching boots crunching over the ice. But this person was both heavier than Margo and moving much more briskly.

"Weiss," the man said in a voice she thought she recognized even through the muffling of his face covering. Fleet Admiral Stowe. "I was told this was urgent. I pray for your sake that's true."

"These are the ones I told you about," Margo said, gesturing to the three of them still on their knees in the ice. Lafayette's knee felt sticky, and she was pretty sure that poke of ice had drawn blood.

"That's your business, not mine," Stowe said. "It makes not a whit of difference to me whether they are inside or outside the ship."

"I would like them to witness its destruction, if that's all right with you," Margo said.

Stowe made an irritated noise. "Your mission parameters are your own business. I don't even care if you're at minimum safe distance or not when the time comes, quite frankly. Just keep them away from my detonation team."

"Yes, sir," Margo said. But even through the muffling layers, Lafayette could hear her disappointment.

"Praise is so hard to get these days," Dieter said in mock sympathy.

Margo said nothing.

"Look, if you want them to stay out on the ice, that's one thing," the man standing behind Lafayette said. "But do we have to stand out here too? We're ship's crew, not Arctic explorers."

"You're dressed warmly enough," Margo said shortly.

More approaching boots, this time from behind them, from the direction of Margo's airship.

"Report," Margo commanded as two parka-clad figures stopped just out of reach of Dieter. They were each about the same height as Margo but moved together with an easy familiarity. Like they'd worked together for years, or maybe even were family members.

"They had quite a lot of some sort of food ration," said one of the parka-clad figures, a woman. "But mostly just books."

"What sorts of books?" Margo asked.

"Handwritten journals. But not like personal diaries. Like..." she trailed off.

"Homework," said her companion, a young man.

"Yeah, like homework," the woman agreed. "What do you want us to do with it?"

Lafayette braced herself for the words "burn it." Only they didn't come. Instead, Margo pondered for a long time before saying, "Stow them in the back. I'll look at them later. See if there's anything of interest to the archivists back in the capital city, maybe."

The woman nodded. She seemed relieved to have at least one fewer task assigned to her.

"You didn't find anything else?" Margo asked.

"You mean besides that fellow's ice axe?" the man asked, gesturing to Dieter.

"No, nothing," the woman said before Margo could respond to that. "Should we have?"

"Apparently not," Margo said shortly.

"Are we heading back then?" the man behind Lafayette asked in a surly tone.

"Not just yet," Margo said. "We're going to watch the demolition first."

"Watch in what sense?" the man shot back. "They're blowing up a ship under the ice, so that it will sink still further under the ice. Frankly, we'd have a better view from inside the airship up at altitude. And we would be warmer."

"And yet we're going to watch from here," Margo said, with just the hint of a commanding tone in her voice. She turned, awkward in the parka, to aim her face first at the man behind Lafayette, then at the woman and her male companion in turn. When none of them made any further objections, she turned to put her back to Lafayette, watching the work of the other crews across the ice.

And so they waited, growing colder by the minute. Lafayette tried to ignore the sticky feeling in her knee, which was growing into an itchy feeling. But that became easier to ignore as her thirst grew into the main focus of her discomfort.

At last the sun lowered down to the western horizon, and the crews on the ice gathered up their equipment and headed back to the gondolas of their airships. The man behind Lafayette was grumbling again, but so low she couldn't make out his words. He wasn't speaking to her, and there was no one else near him. She guessed he was complaining to himself, inside the privacy of his own hood and face covering.

"What happens after this, Margo?" Tristan asked in a soft voice. "Are we going back to the capital city? For… questioning?"

Lafayette had a strong suspicion that the first word he had been about to say had been "interrogation" or maybe even "torture." But he had opted for the gentler word.

At first, Lafayette didn't think Margo was going to answer. But then she turned to stand over them all once more. "No, not to the capital city," she said.

"Where, then?" Tristan asked. "My family doesn't know I'm here."

"Oh, your family knows more than you imagine," Margo said airily. "They've been visited so many times."

"For questioning," Dieter said flatly.

"Well, that, but also for updates on what was known about your activities," Margo said. "You're not wrong to think they're worried. They're very worried. Very worried indeed."

"But we're not going to the capital city, so I'm not going to be able to see them," Tristan said.

"They'll know where you are," Margo said.

"What about Uche Okafo?" Lafayette asked.

"Uche you will see, if only at a distance," Margo said. "You'll be in the same prison, you see. But I doubt they'll let any of you mix with each other. No, that wouldn't be wise at all."

"What prison?" Dieter asked.

"I would answer you," Margo said in a slow drawl. "But I think you all already know the answer to that one. And if you don't... well, I don't want to spoil the surprise."

That could mean only one thing: the island prison was not a rumor.

And they would all be seeing it soon enough.

The airships started lifting off one by one. Lafayette sensed the man behind her shifting his weight from foot to foot, and not out of reaction to the deepening cold. The other two were just within her field of view, talking with their hoods close together, too low for Lafayette to hear.

Finally, Margo turned to the two of them so suddenly they both jumped. "Go, make the ship ready to lift away. We'll be with you momentarily, but probably at a run. Be prepared."

They nodded briskly and then jogged off to the gondola.

The gondola where, Lafayette desperately hoped, Kora was hiding somewhere. She had gone into that impossibly tiny galley, but how had she remained unseen? Lafayette ran over her brief time inside that gondola again and again, but it had all happened so quickly her memories were all a blur.

"Here we go," Margo said, looking up at the twelve airships now circling over the ice floe. "Any moment now, everything you crossed the entire planet to find will be at the bottom of the ocean."

"It's fully functional," Lafayette found herself saying. "Everything has been stripped out of it, but the systems still work. Do you know what that means? Does anyone in the capital city care how much knowledge is about to be lost?"

"You're talking to the exact wrong person about that," Dieter said. "This one burns knowledge when she finds it."

"I had orders," Margo said.

"Both general and specific," Dieter said.

Margo said nothing, but her head pulled back ever so slightly. Like she had taken his words as a blow.

No, that wasn't it. She wasn't hurt. She was surprised.

Dieter had just as good as told her they'd heard the entire conversation she had been having with Central Command. *That*'s what had surprised her.

It might have been wiser to have kept that fact to themselves, but there was nothing to be done about it now.

"Stand them up," Margo said to the man behind Lafayette. But she didn't wait for the feeling of his grabbing hands on her again. She got to her own feet, just noticing the blood-stained hole that punctured her pants below the knee.

Then she felt a rumble through the ice floe below them. Nothing around them looked any different, and yet she knew what must have caused it.

"Here," Margo said, fetching a tablet from one of her parka's large pockets. "These things don't like the cold at all, but it should function long enough to show you…"

She pulled off a mitten to reveal a gloved hand beneath, then tapped at the screen a few times before turning the tablet around to show it to the three of them.

"There's your ship," she said, pointing needlessly at the image of the trapped spaceship shown in a green outline against the blue of the ice. Like Dieter had surmised, the charges themselves had been placed in the ice, and it was cracking away from the ship in long sheets.

"Are we safe here?" the man behind Lafayette asked nervously.

Margo didn't answer. She just watched her own screen upside-down as the ship shifted in its position, but only until a part of the wheel section that had been hung-up on a sheet of ice slid free. Then the entire outline of the ship started sinking, nose first, down into the deep.

"It's rather shallow, this part of the ocean. Only about a kilometer and a half to the bottom," Margo said in a chipper voice. "Probably deeper than you can go, I'm guessing."

"We've seen it. It's gone now. Can we get on the ship and get out of here?" the man behind Lafayette said. It was phrased as a question, but it sounded more like a demand.

"Of course," Margo said, tucking her tablet back into her parka. "Stewart, we've discussed your attitude on many occasions, but I can see there's nothing more that I can say to you about it."

"Glad you noticed," Stewart said even as he pushed Tristan towards the airship, then shoved Lafayette after him.

"Yes, there's nothing for it but to recommend you for a formal repri-mand," Margo said. "Which I can see done the moment we're safely underway."

"Formal reprimand?" Stewart said with a scoff. "You can't do that."

"I've already spoken to my commanding officer about your constant insubordination," Margo said. "He's more than prepared to file the paperwork back at the capital city. You *do* realize that will mean your pay will be docked. All of it."

Stewart didn't answer; he just shoved Lafayette again, so hard she stumbled into the back of Tristan. As if any of this were her fault.

She expected the man to turn on Margo, to either plead his case or really lay into her, to show her his definition of insubordination. But he said nothing, just kept herding them all brutally towards the waiting airship that none of them needed prompting to head to.

Lafayette was just concluding she had misread the situation entirely when they reached the gondola door. Margo hustled to open it for the others, letting Stewart shove Tristan and then Lafayette inside.

Dieter, trailing behind the other two, deftly dodged Stewart's extended hands, stepping into the gondola on his own terms.

But when Margo started to take a step inside herself, Stewart was suddenly there in the doorway, blocking her entry.

"Step aside, pilot," Margo said coldly.

"I don't think so," Stewart said, and shoved her hard in the center of her chest. She stumbled back into the snow, falling on her butt, her hands up in the air in a complete show of startlement.

"Make way!" Stewart yelled towards the cockpit.

"Aye, making way," the woman said.

Lafayette thought she heard the hint of a smile in that woman's tone. Then her companion came out of the cockpit to stand beside Stewart. They both shoved back their hoods and goggles and pulled down their masks. Stewart was pale with long, greasy hair, his gray eyes apparently set in a permanent squint. The other man could've passed for a cousin of the family Lafayette had traveled with to the capital city, all freckles and dark reddish-brown hair.

"Head to the back. Get comfortable. It's a long ride," Stewart said. The man beside him moved ever so slightly. Just enough for them all to see the crossbow he had trained on them.

"To where?" Dieter asked mildly.

"To our just reward," the red-headed man said. And they both laughed.

It wasn't a pleasant laugh.

CHAPTER 24

Lafayette had never wanted to talk to anyone she was sitting right next to so badly as she wanted to talk to Tristan or even Dieter in the hours that followed their departure from the ice floe. But it was impossible to say anything beyond the most benign "Are you okay?" level of discourse, because one of the three crew members was always in the back of the gondola with them, crossbow trained on them all.

They rotated positions far more frequently than Dieter, Tristan and Lafayette had on their own airship. Stewart had disappeared into the galley shortly after they'd left Margo behind and didn't come out again, so Lafayette assumed he was sleeping. But the redheaded man and the woman—who did, indeed, look like she was probably his sister—changed between piloting and guarding the prisoners at the end of every hour.

And neither showed any sign of tiring in their duty.

Which meant that Lafayette couldn't ask the others the important questions. Like if they really thought they were going to the prison island. And if they had any thoughts for a plan to escape. And if that escape would be better executed before or after they reached their destination.

But mostly, Lafayette wanted to ask them if they felt the same as she did. That the little tiff they had just witnessed on the ice had been staged for their benefit.

Which didn't make any sense. What did Margo gain? There had still been airships in the area, and Lafayette was sure she had some way to signal for a pickup. She didn't think Margo was about to freeze to death, alone on the ice floe.

But still, what would be the point of letting these three take off with her prisoners, but without her?

Lafayette couldn't puzzle it out. But she held out hope it made some sense to people from the capital city, who had more experience with Central Planning than she did. Like Tristan and Dieter.

The night dragged on, and despite her best efforts to stay awake, Lafayette caught herself dozing against Tristan's shoulder. But she caught him doing the same against Dieter on even more occasions, so at least they were sharing their lack of alertness.

It had to be closer to dawn than midnight, although the sky outside of the windows was as unrelentingly black as ever. But the whole gondola had a sleepy, quiet quality to it. She could hear Tristan beside her gently snoring, and Dieter beside him was breathing slowly but evenly, like he too was sleeping.

The woman was piloting the airship at the moment, which meant her brother was manning the crossbow. But his eyelids were drooping. His eyes never quite closed, and Lafayette tried to watch for a moment she could take advantage of without being too obvious about it, as she didn't want to draw his attention. Which was a hard needle to thread with so little sleep.

Then she felt something brush up against her side and just stifled a cry of alarm in time to realize it was Kora.

Kora, with a pocket tool in her mouth. She placed it gently in Lafayette's open hand, then retreated back into the darkness between storage crates where she had been hiding.

Lafayette didn't dare look down at what she had in her hand. She just felt around for the correct cutting attachment and then got to work on the plastic band that held her wrists. She kept as still as she could, hoping the man with the crossbow wouldn't notice her hands behind her back were free now. But it was really hard not to give in to the urge to stretch out her arms and get the blood flowing back into her numb hands.

She waited for those eyelids to droop again before sliding closer to Tristan. She put her head on his shoulder, pretending to be asleep even as she groped for his hands. She felt him startle awake at her touch, but he didn't make a sound. It's like he already knew what she was doing.

Once she had his hands free, she pressed the tool into one of them so he could do the same to Dieter.

Dieter's breath changed not at all as Tristan worked at his binds, and Lafayette was afraid he would continue sleeping even past the moment of freedom. But she needn't have worried.

The very instant she heard the soft snap of the binding falling away, Dieter was across the room, knocking the crossbow from the half-conscious man. It wasn't even like he stood up and jumped. It was just like one minute he was asleep on the floor, and the next he was moving with the crossbow already in his hands, shoving the guard back towards Tristan and Lafayette as he charged up to the cockpit.

Lafayette expected some yelp of alarm from the pilot, but she was eerily silent. And the man Tristan was grappling with wasn't so much fighting with him as crushing him with his dead weight. Lafayette rushed to help Tristan get him lowered to the floor, then she sat on their prisoner while Tristan hunted down another set of bindings to zip the man's wrists and ankles together.

The man didn't stir. It was getting more than a little creepy.

"I messed with the air filtration," Kora said as she poked her nose out from her hiding place. "I sneaked into the cockpit from the galley and goosed the valve. I was worried the ship might crash when the pilot went unconscious, but there's so very little wind I told myself it would be okay. And I didn't know what else to do."

"So, there's no oxygen in the cockpit?" Dieter said as he tossed the unconscious woman pilot to Tristan, who was still recovering from having the man thrown at him. He caught her with a grunt and then lowered her to the floor.

"Not so much that, as too much carbon dioxide," Kora said, still sounding deeply regretful. "I was desperate, but it was all I could think to try. My dog brain kept passing out. It's even more susceptible than yours. But I could just manage, with a lot of focus, to keep the body moving around with my construct's commands."

"Kora, you saved us all," Lafayette said, almost awestruck at what the dog had managed. And here Lafayette had thought she had just been hiding in fear of being found and killed by Central Planning.

"It was all I could think to do," Kora said again. But then she gave herself a very doggy sort of shake, ears slapping in a sound that would always bring a smile to Lafayette's face. "I'll go set it back at once. It's dangerous for all of you as it is, and I'm not tall enough to pilot this ship on my own."

"Get to it," Dieter said, far more cheerily than Lafayette felt the moment called for. But then he dove into the galley, still with the crossbow in hand. She heard Stewart make a sleepy complaint that turned into a yelp as his body fell to the floor with a crash.

"That's all crew accounted for," Dieter said after marching Stewart into the back of the gondola.

"So now what?" Lafayette asked. "We do the same rotation of flying, guarding, and resting that they were just doing?"

"I don't like our odds," Tristan said.

"There's someone else on this ship," Stewart said darkly as Dieter bound his wrists.

"What are you saying?" the redheaded man asked, eyes wide. "We picked up some monster from the ice?"

"In a manner of speaking," Kora said as she trotted back into the room. "Although I don't think I'd call myself a *monster*."

"That dog can talk," the woman said in a nervous stammer.

"That dog is half robot," her brother said, eyes even wider than before.

"Right," Dieter said briskly, perching on the crate that was the crossbow guarding position and pointed to each of their three prisoners in turn with the shooting end of that weapon. "We're going to set down here, still on the ice floe, and let you three off."

"We'll die!" the woman gasped.

"No more than *Acting* Special Missions Officer Weiss did," Dieter said, still mimicking the voice of Central Command. "You'll signal for a pickup. You'll be outside for an hour or two, sure, but you'll manage."

"We'll leave you with coffee and peanut butter," Tristan said.

"Oh," Lafayette objected, then flushed red when the other two looked at her. "I wanted the peanut butter."

"We're keeping the peanut butter," Dieter said.

"Fine. Coffee and… I don't know, some of the protein bars we brought from the ship," Tristan said.

"That should work," Dieter said. "Kora, is the cockpit safe now?"

"It should be," Kora said. "Although I did open the grates all the way, so that fresh air is going to be a little extra chilled."

"I'll manage," Dieter said, and shoved the crossbow into Tristan's hands before heading to the cockpit.

Lafayette felt the airship descending beneath her.

"We still have the heading for the prison island, right?" Lafayette said to Tristan. "We have charts to find it? We can get there?"

"If not, we can keep one of these three as navigator," Tristan said.

"We have charts!" Dieter shouted back from the cockpit.

"So we don't need prisoners," Tristan said. Then he broke out into a grin and made an exaggerated sigh of relief. "Thank goodness. Rotating piloting responsibilities is quite enough for me, thank you."

"Plus, we have all the journaling to get back to," Lafayette added.

"Right. Journalling," Tristan agreed. Then he shot a look at the woman on the floor. "Personal diaries. As if."

Lafayette felt her face flushing again but was saved by the sound of harpoons firing, then the lurch as the winches brought them low over the ice.

"Here's your stop," Dieter said as he emerged from the cockpit to open the door. He tossed all three crew members out, one at a time, followed by their coats and the rest of their gear.

"This has the food and coffee in it," Tristan said, gently setting a pack down well clear of their sprawled feet. "It also has a pocket tool. Once you find that, you'll be able to cut yourself free."

"You have a way to send a signal to the other ships, right?" Lafayette asked nervously. She hoped the answer was yes. She didn't know what they'd do if the answer was no.

Stewart started cursing at them, fluently and with great passion. He also started getting up onto his knees, looking like if all he could manage was a head-butt, that was what he would do.

But the woman pushed past him, also on her knees, to say, "Yes. I have a comm. Margo isn't far away."

"Oh, isn't she?" Dieter said darkly. But then he just shrugged, and slammed the door closed.

"We're really just going to leave them there," Tristan said, sounding stunned.

"You heard the lady," Dieter said as he headed back to the cockpit to release the lines to the harpoons. "Margo isn't far away. And Margo strikes me as quite resourceful. They're all fine."

"Are you sure?" Tristan said. But he was looking at Lafayette.

"It felt like a show, didn't it?" Lafayette said to him even as the airship started to lift back up into the air. "Margo was putting on a show for us."

"Okay," Tristan said, sounding unconvinced. "But why? She needs to turn us all in to keep the position she earned by betraying us, right? So why let these three take us away?"

"We're on the fastest ship, faster than anything in the fleet," Lafayette said.

"Yeah, but why not with her?" Tristan persisted.

"Political machinations," Dieter yelled back from inside the cockpit. "Clearly threatening Stewart with a reprimand was all a show. My money is on him being very firmly on her side. But the person she reports to? The one she's supposed to turn us in to? That guy, maybe not so much."

"She's letting us go so her superior can't take the credit?" Tristan said.

"It's a theory," Dieter said, then turned his attention to navigating the ship.

"What I really want to know is, did she plan for us to escape? Or was her plan that her underlings would deliver us to our destination?" Lafayette said.

"In order to answer that, we'd have to know whether or not she knew Kora was on the airship," Tristan said.

They both looked down at the dog. Who was panting in an anxious way.

"Sorry. Not quite recovered," Kora said to them. "This body desperately needs to nap. But maybe some food first?"

"I'm on it," Lafayette said, and dug through her bags for the nutritive paste.

"Did Margo see you?" she asked as she brought the paste in a little bowl to Kora.

"I don't think so," Kora said, then focused all her attention on licking up her food.

"She didn't ask," Tristan said. "She knew we had left the capital city with her, but she didn't ask where she was when she caught us. And somehow, I don't think she just forgot we ought to have Kora with us."

"If only she'd pushed this crew out the door and taken off with us instead of the other way around," Lafayette said. "Then we could ask her all these questions."

"She'd only lie," Tristan said. "She would spin so many lies."

"I've checked the charts," Dieter said from the doorway to the cockpit. "With current conditions, we should reach this island prison in five days. And have you seen what's in the galley? Because we are fully stocked. And not a freeze-dried soup packet in sight."

"So we carry on stuffing ourselves for a few more days," Lafayette said.

Because who knew what lay ahead after they reached their destination. Would they just fall into Central Planning hands again? Or would they finally find a way to get Uche Okafo free?

Did her father get her message? Would there ever be a way for her to get one back from him?

But she pushed all those thoughts from her mind as she went into the galley to help Tristan put together a meal. Because there was one thing she knew for sure.

She would be going into that future with friends at her side.

And where they were going, there wouldn't be snow or ice anywhere. Nothing but warm water and warmer winds under wide blue skies.

That alone would be worth the fight to get there.

CHECK OUT BOOK FOUR

History sleeps beneath them all, and she will wake it.

Lafayette Eloi used to live the life of an ordinary girl in an ordinary village. But she left that life behind to follow her father on his quest to uncover their planet's past. Namely, the remains of a crashed starship that proved none of them belonged on this world.

His quest ended with him trapped on a spaceship in orbit around their world. But her path carried her on, across bandit-ridden grasslands to the capital city in search of a second crashed ship. Only nothing in the capital was as it seemed, and she was nearly ensnared in political intrigue she scarcely understood when her quest came to the attention of the mysterious governmental forces known only as Central Planning.

Then her path took her to the top of the world, to a polar ice floe that hid the remains of a third ship, perfectly preserved in the ice. But the too-sudden arrival of Central Planning airships cut short her time on that ship, and she and her friends barely escaped with their lives.

They are free once more, riding the winds in a stolen airship. But her quest has barely begun. Because at the end of this airship journey, she hopes to find the remains of a fourth ship. Only this one will be the hardest to reach of all.

Because it lies on the bottom of the ocean.

Foraging the Hidden Sanctuary, Book 4 of The Forgotten Planet YA sci-fi series, available April 7, 2026 direct from me or May 12, 2026 in stores everywhere.

SCI-FI SERIAL PODCAST!

Check out my new monthly podcast of serialized science fiction: THE TALES OF THE CHAI MAKHANI TRIO!

Elyot loathes the massive Commonwealth ships that hover menacingly over his home world of Adghal. He hates the Commonwealth enforcers who harass the populace even more. But with his mother missing and presumed dead, Elyot keeps his head down and strives to avoid notice. And he succeeds until the day two strangers enter his life...

New episodes of this sci-fi serial drop every 1st of the month.

Now streaming on Apple Podcasts, Google Podcasts, Spotify, Stitcher and more. Also available in eBook and print everywhere books or sold. For a complete episode listing, check out the page on my website.

COMPLETE SERIES: THE TRAVELS OF SCOUT SHANNON

The complete six-book series THE TRAVELS OF SCOUT SHANNON begin with book one, Under Falling Skies.

Scout Shannon's whole family died the day the Space Farers dropped an asteroid on their domed city. Now she lives alone, out in the wild with only her dogs for company. She prefers it that way.

But Scout finds herself at a crossroads. One road leads back to a quiet life snug under the protective dome of a city. The other road leads to a life in the rebellion, a life of adventure and excitement but also danger. Dare she try to find the rebels hiding in the hills?

Then a chance encounter with a stranger from the other side of the galaxy threatens to derail what remains of Scout's life. The entire galaxy awaits her, if she survives the next four days.

"Under Falling Skies", a young adult science fiction novel, set on a remote planet with a distinctly Old West feel. For fans of gunslinging women and young girl assassins. And dogs.

Under Falling Skies, the first book in THE TRAVELS OF SCOUT SHANNON, available everywhere now.

COMPLETE SERIES: THE RITCHIE AND FITZ SCI-FI MURDER MYSTERIES

The Ritchie and Fitz Sci-Fi Murder Mysteries starts with Murder on the Intergalactic Railway.

For Murdina Ritchie, acceptance at the Oymyakon Foreign Service Academy means one last chance at her dream of becoming a diplomat for the Union of Free Worlds. For Shackleton Fitz IV, it represents his last chance not to fail out of military service entirely.

Strange that fate should throw them together now, among the last group of students admitted after the start of the semester. They had once shared the strongest of friendships. But that all ended a long time ago.

But when an insufferable but politically important woman turns up murdered, the two agree to put their differences aside and work together to solve the case.

Because the murderer might strike again. But more importantly, solving a murder would just have to impress the dour colonel who clearly thinks neither of them belong at his academy.

Murder on the Intergalactic Railway, the first book in the Ritchie and Fitz Sci-Fi Murder Mysteries.

ALSO FROM KATE MACLEOD

Love heists and capers? Then check out my new series, THE VIC HARPER CAPERS. The action starts with the novella THE THIRD POLE JOB.

Vic Harper and her gang retired wealthy from their life of thievery and heists. Whether in a luxury condo overlooking the river in Minneapolis or in a modernist mansion built into the side of a mountain in Colorado, life comes easy now.

Perhaps too easy.

When an old friend asks for a favor his niece, Vic and her mentor Chase Woodward leap at the chance to relieve a little of the boredom. But a quick bit of B&E in a wealthy suburb of Chicago leads to an even greater challenge.

The prize? Nothing much. Just the opportunity to level a playing field for their friend's niece.

But the heist? May prove to be their toughest ever. Because to get to the prize, they'll have to climb a mountain.

And not just any mountain. Their prize waits on the summit of Mount Everest.

THE THIRD POLE JOB, the first novella in the Vic Harper Caper series. For those who love capers, heists and other impossible missions.

ALSO FROM RATATOSKR PRESS

Also from Ratatoskr Press, The Witches Three Cozy Mystery Series by Cate Martin, a mix of mystery and magic that begins with Book 1: Charm School.

Amanda Clarke thinks of herself as perfectly ordinary in every way. Just a small-town girl who serves breakfast all day in a little diner nestled next to the highway, nothing but dairy farms for miles around. She fits in there.

But then an old woman she never met dies, and Amanda was named in her will. Now Amanda packs a bag and heads to the big city, to Miss Zenobia Weekes' Charm School for Exceptional Young Ladies. And it's not in just any neighborhood. No, she finds herself on Summit Avenue in St. Paul, a street lined with gorgeous old houses, the former homes of lumber barons, railroad millionaires, even the writer F. Scott Fitzgerald. Why, Amanda can practically hear the jazz music still playing across the decades.

Scratch that. The music really, literally, still plays in the backyard of the charm school. Because the house stretches across time itself. Without a witch to protect this tear in the fabric of the world, anything can spill over. Like music.

Or like murder.

The complete series is out now, and it all starts with Charm School.

FREE EBOOK!

Like exclusive, free content?

To get two prequel short stories to THE RITCHIE AND FITZ SCI-FI MURDER MYSTERIES as well as a bonus prequel novelette to the completed six-book series THE TRAVELS OF SCOUT SHANNON, signup for my monthly newsletter at KateMacLeodWrites.com.

Thank you!

ABOUT THE AUTHOR

Kate MacLeod has written stories which have appeared in Analog, Strange Horizons and Mythic Delirium, among other places. She is also the author of two young adult science fictions series: The Travels of Scout Shannon, and The Ritchie and Fitz Sci-Fi Murder Mysteries. She also contributes to a serialized science fiction podcast called The Tales of the Chai Makhani Trio. She currently lives in Minneapolis, Minnesota.

Find out more about the author and sign up for her newsletter at KateMacLeodWrites.com.

ALSO BY KATE MACLEOD

Novels

The Slums of the Solar System:

Mitwa

The Mars of Malcontents

The Whole World for Each

Books 1-3 Box Set

The Travels of Scout Shannon:

Under Falling Skies

In Quaking Hills

Among Treacherous Stars

Against Impassable Barriers

Over Freezing Altitudes

At Galactic Central

The Travels of Scout Shannon Books 1-3

The Travels of Scout Shannon Books 4-6

The Travels of Scout Shannon Books 1-6

The Ritchie and Fitz Sci-Fi Murder Mysteries:

Murder on the Intergalactic Railway

Murder in the Skies

Body in the Catacombs

Death on the Summit

An Undiplomatic Murder

A Lethal Betrayal

The Ritchie and Fitz Sci-Fi Murder Mysteries Books 1-3

The Ritchie and Fitz Sci-Fi Murder Mysteries Books 4-6

The Forgotten Planet

Raiding the Forgotten Derelict

Plundering the Planetary Secrets

Salvaging the Arctic Wreck

Foraging the Hidden Sanctuary

Sci-Fi Novellas

The Intergenerational Tree

I Rise into a Daybreak

Caper Novellas

The Third Pole Job

The Twelve Days of Christmas Job

10-Story Collections

Tales of Blood and Ink

Tales of Old Gods and New

Tales of Spaceships and Magic

5-Story Collections

Tales from Heian-Kyo and Others

Tales from the Edges and Ends

Tales from Forgotten Days

Tales from Ancient and Future Times

Tales From Across Space

Tales from Places Strange and Familiar